STRYPH

HELLISH #9

CHARITY PARKERSON

--Warning: This book is intended for readers over the age of 18.

Copyright © 2019 Charity Parkerson
Editor: Vicky Reese
ISBN: 978-1-946099-53-2

INTRODUCTION

STRYPH IS NEITHER GOOD NOR BAD. MEETING
AMOR IS ABOUT TO TEST THAT.

As one of Heaven's weapons, Stryph walks alone. He has no soul to share. Considered neither good nor bad, Stryph keeps life's balance. Every living being depends on his neutrality. It's an existence that moved beyond weary several millennia ago. His only friend, Shepherd has found his mates. Now, Stryph's longing for a nonexistent mate is twice as strong. It's a predicament Goddess Celeste has a plan to fix.

Amor hates everyone equally, which is funny because he's literally love. Being sent to Earth to deal with things he doesn't care about, does nothing to improve Amor's bitterness. But Amor loves Celeste, and it's been years since he's visited the watery planet that's survived so many fits from darker gods.

He plans to treat the trip like a vacation. Amor never expects Stryph.

When these two powerful and volatile beings meet, the explosion of emotions is real. Only time will tell what those feelings turn out to be. It could be love, hate, or simply lust. Or maybe they'll just end the world.

ONE

RAFF'S POOL Hall was a small but bustling bar in the middle of werewolf country. The place was always filled to the brim with wolves in human clothing. They looked like everyday people. They walked and talked like normal men and women, but they were animals to their core. Still Stryph preferred to spend his time among them over any other species. He was especially fond of this pack. Raff's pack. His love of the southeast wolves had nothing to do with their leader. It was their pack master's mate that called to Stryph. Well, one of his mates—Shepherd.

Shepherd was over six feet of muscle. He was blond-haired and blue-eyed with a heart so beautiful it was blinding. The human was the only man Stryph had ever run across who had both a vampire and a werewolf mate. The throuple stoked his longtime jealousy over being forever alone. Stryph was a heavenly weapon. He had no soul to share with anyone. There was no one out there for him. All he had was sex. Hardcore, dirty, kinky sex. To a lot of men that would sound like nirvana—an eternity of nameless, faceless fucking. Anyone who'd lived as long as Stryph knew differently. It was a lonely existence. Years turned into centuries. Centuries became millennia. All alone. The silence was deafening. Maddening. So, Stryph spent a lot of time here at Raff's—people watching and dreaming.

Stryph sank the eight ball in the corner pocket. Honestly, he didn't like pool all that much. It was one of a million things that had gotten old over the endless years. But the game killed time, because the one thing Stryph never did was interact. Not here. Once again, Shepherd was the only exception. Unfortunately, Shepherd wasn't here yet. Stryph's boredom spiked to an all-time high.

He scanned the room, hoping he'd spot Shepherd coming through the door. Stryph knew he wouldn't. He always felt Shepherd before he saw him. Another figure caught Stryph's attention instead. Stryph's stomach growled. Tiny and blond, the guy might've gotten lost in the crowd if not for his vibe. Power radiated around him. The slight golden glow to his skin was undetectable to the human eye. But Stryph was born of the heavens. He could see what others could not—like the light of a heavenly being. That was new in Raff's. Even though no one else would be able to see the guy's glow, people still watched him. Each person he passed stared hard at him until he moved on, then they moved closer to their mates, or starting hunting for one. It was fucking odd.

Stryph found himself following the guy. His curiosity piqued. Most gods didn't tend to come here often. A single planet was a little too small for their tastes. But there was no denying the pulse of power emanating from this one. As if the guy felt his pursuit, his head turned Stryph's way. Emerald green eyes that reflected the light caught and held his stare. Stryph lost his breath. The guy looked away, dismissing Stryph. A smirk pulled at Stryph's lips. The game was on.

The man looked as if he searched the crowd for someone in particular. Stryph used that knowledge to his advantage, sidling into the man's space. "You look lost. Now, you're found. Stryph at your service," he said with a slight bow.

Nothing. No smile or reaction of any sort crossed his perfect features. He was fucking flawless. "I know what you are."

Stryph's humor doubled. "Unfair," he cried, being as obnoxious as possible. "I don't have the curse of seeing into the future. You have the advantage in every way. Can I not—at least—know your name?"

A long, loud huff escaped the tiny sprite. He stared up at Stryph, visibly fighting an eye roll. "Amor."

Goosebumps rose on Stryph's skin. It was no wonder he'd been instantly enthralled, and the crowd was restless as hell for a mate. When Stryph found his voice, it came out sounding heavy with lust. There was no stopping it. "Well, now. It's not every day I'm blessed with love's presence."

Amor failed at keeping his expression blank. He sneered and still he was sexy. "I'm a little busy at the moment. Please step aside."

Without budging, Stryph slowly looked right and then left before focusing on Amor again. He lowered his voice to a stage whisper, as if he didn't want to speak loudly and embarrass Amor. "This is a bar. People don't come here when they're busy."

Amor leaned in and matched Stryph's obnoxious tone. "I'm not a person." He winked slowly, leaving no doubt he meant to be an ass. "Don't tell anyone."

Stryph's cheeks hurt from smiling. He straightened, fully intent on behaving and keeping Amor off balance. "Seriously, though, you look lost. Do you need help finding someone?"

For a full minute, Amor eyed him in silence. Finally, he shook his head and sighed. "Do you know Celeste's grandson, Jonathan?"

Against his will, Stryph's smile tightened. Amor would be looking for someone who didn't care for Stryph, which really, that was a long list. "As it happens, I do."

Some of the confrontation left Amor's features. "Ah, good. Celeste sent me to see him for... reasons. Unfortunately, I couldn't zap into his exact area. I've been driving around these back roads for hours without luck. Someone mentioned I might find him here."

"You won't find him here." Stryph didn't pull any punches. "He doesn't leave his property often, since he's busy, and no longer looks the least bit human. I could take you to him."

Amor straightened his gray t-shirt, as if it had invisible wrinkles. The move had the material molding to a set of perfect abs. "Directions will suffice."

Stryph glanced around. His mind raced. He couldn't let Amor get away. Not yet. He met Amor's gaze once more. He fought the urge to flirt and have his way. Dark urges clawed at his brain. Amor was immortal. He could take abuse. "Let me walk you out. Too many beings with immaculate hearing in this place."

Amor surveyed the room and nodded. "True. It's always best to be careful when protecting royalty."

Truthfully, Stryph didn't give two fucks about Jonathan or his safety. He simply wanted to buy some more time and get Amor alone. Stryph motioned Amor toward the door. The moment he passed, Stryph set his hand on the small of Amor's back, and steered him outside. Amor didn't jump away or threaten Stryph with the loss of limb. Stryph took it as a win. "Where is your car?"

"There," Amor said, nodding toward a pearl-white BMW.

Stryph bit back a laugh. What else would Cupid drive? The doors automatically unlocked as they approached. Stryph opened the driver's side door for

Amor—like the gentleman he wasn't. "Turn right from the lot. Drive nine miles until you come to an iron gate. You're there." He tapped the roof of the car, ensuring it wouldn't start.

Amor dipped his chin. "I appreciate your help. It won't be forgotten."

"Always at your service. Maybe after you finish your business with Jonathan, you could come back and have a drink with me?"

"Maybe."

Stryph's lips twitched along with his cock. Amor had spunk, and it wasn't every day he had a shot at luring the god of love to bed. That had to be hot. "Then I should get out of your way so you can hurry back."

With a nod, Amor slid behind the wheel. Stryph closed the door behind him and stepped back. As planned, the car didn't start. The door flew open. Green eyes latched on to him and flashed with rage. Stryph immediately recognized his misstep. Amor might've returned and gave him a chance if Stryph hadn't done anything to his car. Not now. Now they were done. Stryph might not make it out with his skin intact.

"Do you need a ride?" Stryph asked, determined to brazen it out.

"Was that your plan? Did you fuck with my car to shove your company on me?"

Stryph held up his hands and shook his head. "You're a god. All you have to do is snap your fingers and your car will be fine. In fact, you can go anywhere you want in the blink of an eye without a car. Why would I bother messing with your car?"

Amor pulled himself up to his full five feet and six inches and went toe to toe with Stryph. "I told you I was busy. Yet you still *fucked with my car*, and for your information, I like driving. It's fun. None of that is the point right now."

"Okay." Even Stryph heard the confusion in his voice. "What is the point?"

Amor poked him in the chest. "The point is that you tried to force your company on me. If I was a human, I'd been stuck. The point is, you were wrong for that. Plus, you messed with *my* stuff." His gaze moved around the parking lot. His irises glowed for a second before an evil smile pulled at his lips. He stepped around Stryph and made a beeline for Stryph's Chiron. Money meant nothing to Stryph, but still. A hint of horror struck him. An angry god might do anything. Several feet away, Amor stopped. His arms lifted into an archery stance. A golden bow appeared in his hands from thin air. An arrow cut through the air, puncturing Stryph's front tire. "There. Now you can waste your time snapping your fingers too."

Stryph shook his head. "Be honest," Stryph said dryly. "It's little man syndrome, isn't it? Is that what's wrong with you?"

"I don't know. Is it tiny dick disease? Is that what's wrong with you?"

Stryph shrugged. "Let's fuck and then you'll know."

Amor narrowed his eyes at Stryph. "Okay."

At Amor's response, Stryph's mind blanked. He hadn't truly expected his proposition to get accepted. Nor did Amor wear the expression of a man who'd just accepted a proposition. "Fine."

"Fine," Amor repeated as he stormed back to his car. With a snap of his fingers, the car fired to life. He slammed the door behind him when he climbed in.

Stryph's irritation melted away, replaced with humor. He had a feeling he'd just been played. That was new. He imagined Amor planned to keep him waiting all night, with no intentions of returning. With a snap of his fingers, Stryph's tire was back to normal.

Amor's window came down. His angry stare locked on to Stryph. "Well, are you coming or not?"

Stryph leapt to comply. There was no way he'd miss a night with Amor and his fiery temper. True passion was rarer than people realized. Even if Amor destroyed Stryph in the process, Stryph couldn't wait for such a beautiful death.

TWO

THE HOUSE WAS quiet for once. It was as if every being under Jonathan's roof had decided to stay in bed tonight. Like love was in the air. Jonathan felt it. His sexy mates kept snuggling closer until he was squashed between them. Jonathan couldn't get enough. He didn't need air to survive, which was a good thing. His two massive warriors didn't know the strength of their hugs.

"Och, I donae want to move," Niall moaned against Jonathan's throat. His hand slid across Jonathan's stomach, making Jonathan painfully hard.

"Mhmm," Cin hummed against Jonathan's hair, as if that was the extent of the energy he had to spare.

"What if we just stayed here in bed and never moved? Do you think anyone would notice?"

"They'd notice," Niall said, answering Jonathan. "We could try anyway."

"Mhmm," Cin hummed again. "Have I told you both how much I love you lately? I'm getting to a point where I don't want to do anything else but be right here with you."

It was Jonathan's turn to hum. "Mhmm. Same."

"Agreed," Niall said, snuggling closer. "My sexy babies. My whole world."

Yeah, they weren't moving anytime soon. His hands found their way beneath his men's kilts. This was heaven.

STEAM FILLED THE BATHROOM, MAKING THE AIR thick. Lire couldn't get enough of his men. He knew they should be out on patrol, relieving the wolves for the night. He couldn't stop trying to please his mates. Dougal pulled his hair, riding Lire's tongue and pounding at his throat while Faolan thrust slow and deep inside him. If he was human, he'd already be dead from exhaustion or heart failure after the massive number of orgasms his sexy men had pulled from him already. As a sex demon, he was definitely well fed. As a bonded male, he was well satiated. Moans and other delicious sounds echoed from the walls. Love completely owned Lire. He should be fine to stop, but he couldn't. His mind was soaked with love and pleasure. Nothing held a hint of interest to him except being right here. It should've seemed odd, but it was his mates. No one had been more blessed than him. He'd been given the sexiest of men. They'd been handed an eternity together. His eyes stung. It was beautiful.

THE AIR LEFT RISK'S LUNGS. ONLY THE TINY blond angel currently straddling his hips moved Risk to the point of stealing his breath. It had always been this way. The sight of Tam's pale skin against Risk's dark body was fascinating to him. There was no one else for him. Goddess Celeste had chosen his fated mate beautifully. She was the wisest of all the gods. Each time he looked at Tam, Risk's heart overflowed with love. His body burned. Tam's gentle lovemaking made Risk's eyes sting. He loved Tam so much sometimes it overwhelmed him.

"I love you." Tam sounded breathless and every

bit as moved as Risk felt tonight. He also looked turned on and ready to go all night.

Risk couldn't take it any longer. He rolled, tucking Tam beneath him. Risk claimed Tam's lips as he rocked inside his sexy mate. "I love you too. So much," Risk gasped between kisses. His lips moved to Tam's jaw. His heart needed more. "Stay in bed with me tonight. Let's lock out the world and focus on us. I don't want to share."

"Yes." Tam's short fingernails dug into Risk's shoulders. He strained against Risk, proving how close he was to coming. Risk already knew he wouldn't stop. Even once he secured Tam's orgasm, Risk planned to keep going. He wanted everything his perfect mate had to give. Otherwise, the love that kept growing inside him might choke him.

AN ODDLY PEACEFUL SILENCE FILLED THE CAR after Amor's rage bled away. It had been an interesting night so far. Amor never would've expected it to be peaceful spending time with Stryph, especially after their spat. It didn't make sense. Stryph was discord in the literal sense. Yet Amor was content to the point of fighting the urge to purr. That was probably due to Stryph also being sex on two legs. He dripped sensuality. It wasn't easy being him. Amor stayed in the heavens because things were muted there. Otherwise, it was hard for him to endure himself, and no one could tolerate being with him for more than one night. Even that long was dangerous unless they were powerful in their own right. Love was a beautiful thing between most. Weak minds and spirits twisted that powerful adoration into ugly jealousy and obsession. Stryph, while obviously selfish, wouldn't need or want Amor past tonight. That sounded good to him. It had been a damn long time since anyone had fucked him without strings. Stryph would.

The iron gate Stryph told him about came into view. It was a tall archway over a driveway. He slowed to check it out. Only one word twisted the iron: *Hellish*. A smile touched Amor's lips. It looked like Stryph had been honest. He'd led Amor directly to the Hellish clan. Not everything Stryph said had been a trick.

"Well, they're not hiding, are they?" Even Amor heard the humor in his voice.

Stryph's eerie light gray gaze swung his way. The night made them iridescent. "They don't need to, do they? Nephilims are stronger than their sires.

Jonathan is Goddess Celeste's grandson." Stryph didn't expound. He didn't need to. Goddess Celeste was the strongest of the gods. As her grandson, Jonathan could likely end quite a few worlds with the snap of his fingers. Amor hoped the man's heart was as pure as his grandmother's. He kind of liked this watery planet.

Amor steered his car down the drive. The instant he passed beneath the iron arch, wolves appeared on either side of his car, sprinting alongside him. They stuck to him all the way to the house. The sprawling mansion was worthy of Jonathan's position. Gorgeous landscaping surrounded the gigantic brick home. Tons of flowers and trees, including a huge willow with branches that draped all the way to the ground. It was a lovely place. Amor parked and killed the engine.

Stryph grabbed for the door handle. He flashed a humorous look Amor's way. "Get ready to be bombarded by the world's most adorable wolves that somehow landed the prestigious position of guards. Don't shoot them like you did my tire."

With an eye roll he felt to his core, Amor slipped from the car. The black and silver wolves that had been flanking his car transformed from beasts to men in the flash of an eye. The black wolf became a dark-haired and light eyed beauty, while the silver wolf became a man with long, silver hair. Not a single line marred his face, but his spirit felt much older than the boy wolf. Yet, they were mates. Amor would know.

The silver haired man gave a short bow. "Amor, this is a surprise. What brings you our way?"

Ah, wolves and their keen sense of smell. He'd never been able to hide his identity from them. "Goddess Celeste."

Silver hair's gaze sharpened. "In that case," he said, motioning toward the door. "My mate, Evan, will alert the king."

With an adorable smile, meant only for his mate, he reached for Evan's hand. They linked fingers and headed for the door. Amor followed. He didn't particularly care for a majority of people or creatures, but he couldn't help but smile at the pair. He'd done good work here. There was pride in watching love thrive. Celeste might pair the souls, but mates didn't always love one another. They needed Amor for that.

Stryph stroked the small of Amor's back, reminding Amor of his presence. It occurred to him, the pair hadn't greeted Stryph, but neither had he been turned away. In truth, he'd been treated like he was invisible. That tidbit was something to muse over later.

Inside, the home was lovely and obviously lived in. There were signs of life everywhere he looked. An abandoned coffee cup on the end table. Shoes near the door. Before Amor had time to take things in, two huge warriors and a demon greeted them. These were the guards he'd been expecting outside. While the demon wore all black, matching his long black hair, his mates wore only kilts. All three were heavily armed. Their weapons were useless against him, but still. He appreciated their diligence.

"The king will be with you momentarily."

Amor dipped his chin, acknowledging the demon's claim. He was beyond curious how their king knew of his presence since Evan hadn't announced him, as the silver wolf had claimed he would.

"Jonathan knows everything," a tiny blond guy said, appearing from a side door. His mate followed him, guarding him as if he held some seat of importance.

Amor's gaze sharpened on the boy. "You heard my thoughts."

The boy took a step back into the shelter of his mate's arms. "Sorry."

"Don't be sorry," Amor said, keeping his voice soothing and blatantly using his gift of charm against him. He only hoped to sooth an obviously battered and tired spirit.

The boy toyed with a doll filled with magic. "You're a god."

"I am." Amor smiled. The boy had a sweet soul. It was nearly blinding in its beauty.

"I'm Tam," Tam said with a shy smile. "This is my mate, Risk."

Amor nodded toward them both. "It's nice to meet you."

Tam motioned toward the wolves. "This is Evan and Bleidd."

Amor took in every name and filed it away.

"Those three," Tam said, pointing toward the guards. "are Lire, Dougal, and Faolan."

Each time Amor looked away from Tam, he shuffled closer. Amor found himself purposely looking elsewhere to see how close he'd come. It was adorable.

"Hi, Stryph," Tam said, sounding bright and every bit as welcoming to him as he had with Amor. Amor smiled at his kindness.

"Hello, sweet angel."

Amor's smile grew at Stryph's greeting. No

matter his purpose in life, Stryph had goodness inside him too. Amor felt it.

Three men filed in, changing the air in the room. It popped and sizzled with power. The hair stood on Amor's arms. The first man was huge and dangerous looking. Amor recognized him as Niall, the son of the late king of Scotland. They'd met. Bringing up the rear, Jonathan's second mate. He was every bit as strong as Niall. Once again. Celeste had been on her game while choosing soul mates. But Amor's gaze wouldn't budge from the creature flanked by the Scots. He was taller than both his mates. He glowed brighter than a god while his eyes swirled like potted gold. Black wings practically dragged the floor behind him. Stryph was right. Jonathan couldn't pass for human. He wore the same kilt as his clan. Unlike his stone-faced clansmen, Jonathan smiled. He was terrifying and comforting at the same time. Amor had the advantage of being able to see his soul. He was pure and good. Amor felt moved to be in his presence. Celeste had much to be proud of in this home.

"Evan tells me you were sent by my grandmother. I believe you're the first messenger she's ever sent."

No one sat or offered him a seat. Amor got the

impression they were still assessing his motives. "She's too important to the heavens for this world. No offense. The heavens are much larger and more important to the existence of all than one planet. While she can visit in very brief bursts, it's not safe for her to do so. This was the best she could do tonight." Amor didn't waste anyone's time. "I am Amor."

"Ah," the demon Lire said, dragging out the word. "This explains the mood in our home tonight." His mates nodded.

Amor fought a smile. His presence alone would affect the hearts of everyone for miles. While humans would feel—mostly—restless, for creatures as powerful as the ones living in this place, Amor's influence would be magnified a thousand-fold. Amor didn't substantiate Lire's claim. Like all gods, he didn't list his powers or weaknesses. Instead, he stayed focused on Jonathan. "Celeste hates that she cannot come in person to help celebrate your birthday."

"Oh, ha," Jonathan said, turning even brighter. "I forgot. Things have been crazy," he added before Amor could ask. Not that Amor needed to question Jonathan's words. Being immortal was endless. Each year slid into another until time no longer mattered.

Age and the marking of passing time eventually got away from all eternal creatures.

Instead of getting into a philosophical discussion of time, Amor snapped his fingers. A brightly wrapped box appeared in his hands. "Celeste sends her love." Niall accepted the gift and passed it Jonathan's way, as if he wouldn't allow Amor to get closer to his mate. Amor might've been insulted if he didn't understand exactly how important Jonathan was to the world.

As Jonathan opened the card on his gift, a light brush of fingers down his arm distracted Amor. He was more than a little surprised to find Tam had been the one to touch him. It seemed the boy had finally managed the courage to close the final distance between them. He looked embarrassed by his own actions.

He blushed. "Sorry. You're very shiny. It was like I was a moth, I guess." His blush deepened on the confession.

Amor's cheeks ached from smiling. He truly didn't like most anyone, but this one... he was special. "It's okay. You can't hurt me."

Tam nodded. His light blue gaze stayed locked on Amor. "Is it okay if I ask you a dumb question?"

"Of course." Tam was the only one who'd

acknowledged Stryph. That bought him favor in Amor's books.

"Why are you so short?" He immediately looked nervous and started wringing his doll again. "I didn't mean that as an insult. I'm small too. It's just that most of the powerful beings I've met are huge and tower over me. I mean, Stryph is massive. So, why are you short?"

Amor bit the inside of his cheek to keep from laughing. The humor showed in his voice when he leaned Tam's way and spoke softly—like he had a secret. "The most powerful beings, like you and I, are always made tiny, so all the other powerful beings are forced to bow to us." He cast a look around and chuckled when all the men in the room suddenly straightened their spines, as if they realized they were doing exactly as Amor accused—bowing to hear them better.

Tam giggled. He brought the doll to his lips, stifling the sound, but his eyes shone bright with his humor. Amor couldn't stop smiling. This one was the key to Hell. Amor saw it now. He was such a glorious choice that Amor felt humbled by the combined powers of the gods. This was incorruptible while, by all accounts, looking like the least likely candidate. No evil entity would ever suspect him.

Amor decided he could show that he was also a case of being more than met the eye. "I'm also a creature of heaven." He let his great gray wings unfurl. His clothes transformed into lightweight golden armor. "A general of the soldiers of heaven. Powerful in my own right."

"Oh, wow," Tam gasped, petting the wing closest to him. "You're so pretty."

Amor's eyebrows rose. In his true form, most didn't think he was pretty. He was a warrior of heaven. Warriors weren't pretty. Before he could think of a thing to say, Jonathan gasped, bringing Amor's gaze his way.

"What the actual fuck?" Jonathan sounded comically outraged. "He has," he almost bounced in place as he waved his hands and visibly struggled to find his words. "fucking magic clothes," he finally yelled. "I have wings too and they destroy everything I've ever tried to wear. But you just went from a shirt to armor. Can you go back?"

Amor immediately reverted to his earlier form—clothes and all.

"Shut your whore mouth," Jonathan yelled, startling a laugh from Amor. No one had ever spoken to him like Jonathan, but he could tell the man wasn't being insulting. Jonathan was merely irritated. "How are you doing that? I want clothes."

The whine in his voice had Amor's humor kicking up a notch. "You're not human. Stop shopping in human stores."

Jonathan clutched the gift box to his chest, looking ready to pop. "There are different stores? Are you screwing with me?"

"I will take you sometime," Stryph said, speaking up for the first time. "There are many places where I live for beings such as yourself. If your mates allow it, I would be happy to show you."

Jonathan nodded. "Thank you, Stryph. I would really like that."

He sounded so close to crying, Amor wondered if anyone had bothered to instruct Jonathan on anything since his powers evolved, or if he'd been left to muddle through alone.

"Of course, your majesty." Stryph seemed sincere. Amor found his gaze sliding Stryph's way. He was incredibly sexy—like a Viking of old. His blond hair was shaved on the sides but long in the center. He kept it pulled back away from his face. But it was the man's unnaturally light gray eyes that held Amor's attention. He stared back at Amor without blinking. Stryph didn't possess a drop of human blood. In fact, he didn't have blood at all. No heart beat in his chest. He was a weapon with a conscience. Designed for a purpose. Power thrummed from him. Amor was a good eighty percent sure he'd underestimated Stryph upon their first meeting, but he still wanted Stryph with something akin to desperation. This chore couldn't be done quickly enough. Stryph would ensure Amor felt him for days afterward. His mouth watered at the thought.

"This is such an amazing gift," Jonathan cooed, bringing Amor's focus his way. "Oh my god. They smell like chocolate." He brought the pot of exotic flowers that couldn't be found in the mortal world to his nose.

"They're from my personal garden. You don't need to do anything for them. They'll never die here. This house is too full of love. That's their natural food. Now," Amor said, motioning toward the flowers. "To ensure they thrive here, Celeste has also ordered a full week of rest for your household. She's set safeguards in place to make sure the world is fine while you relax. Spend some time with your mates. All of you." Amor cast a look around the room, focusing for a split second on everyone who lived there. "The more you revel in your mates this week, the more the plant will thrive. I'm staying in this realm for the next week too, so you probably won't be able to resist each other anyhow." A chuckle that sounded evil even to Amor's ears sneaked out as he made the confession.

"Oh, please stay here with us," Tam begged. "I'd love to get to know you."

"I'll be back," Amor promised. His gaze slid Risk's way. "For now, your mate seems very hungry. You should feed him."

Tam blushed but scurried closer to Risk, as if he couldn't wait to assuage that desire.

Amor nodded satisfied. "If I'm needed for any reason between visits, I'm sure you can reach me at Stryph's."

At his claim, Stryph stepped closer and set his hand on the small of Amor's back. Goosebumps rose on Amor's skin. He was so ready to get fucked—hard. Sex and love went hand in hand, making Amor's appetite unabashedly larger than life. He'd existed too long to feel ashamed for taking any partner he chose.

Jonathan moved closer, taking Amor by surprise. He hugged Amor. "Thank you for this. I know you were only the messenger, but it means a lot to us to have you visit. Tam is right. We'd love to get to know you. Come back and spend some time with us before you leave."

"I will." Amor shocked himself with the sincerity in his promise. He would come back. These beings were different from most. They possessed something pure. Amor wanted to know them better. Maybe in getting to know them, he would learn something new about himself. It had been a millennium since anything surprised him. He couldn't wait to see what happened next.

THREE

A DARK HUNGER stirred in Stryph's gut. Patience wasn't his strong point. After watching Amor transform into his warrior form, Stryph was twice as certain Amor could handle him. He couldn't stop setting his hand on the small of Amor's back, staking his claim. It didn't matter that everyone inside Jonathan's was mated. This one was his.

It took longer than Stryph liked to leave Jonathan's. The fact that Jonathan seemed genuinely interested in spending time with Stryph kept him from attempting to steal Amor from their clutches. Each time Amor's sexy emerald gaze swung his way, Stryph suppressed a shiver. There was promise in Amor's stare. He would draw blood.

All hints of pretend patience disappeared as

Stryph ate Amor alive with his gaze on the way to the car. He overcame Amor, crowding him against the driver's side door. Stryph didn't doubt for a second Amor let it happen. That one thought alone made Stryph's dick hard. His lips skimmed Amor's neck. Tam was right. Amor was tiny. It was strange to think of him as a god. The power pulsing from him was unlike any Stryph had touched before. It was tantalizing.

"You should let me kiss you."

Musical laughter caressed Stryph's ears. Amor turned in his arms. His eyes sparkled with good humor as he stared up at Stryph. "Since I'm about to let you do a whole lot more, I don't see why I would balk at a kiss."

Stryph shuffled even closer. His darkness grew to match Amor's light. "Once I'm given permission, I'm likely to take control of way more than you expect."

A sexy sounding hum vibrated from Amor. "That sounds a lot like a dare. I've never backed down from one of those. You should definitely kiss me."

The final word barely left Amor's lips before Stryph claimed Amor's mouth. He wouldn't give Amor time to change his mind. Permission had been given. *Oh, fuck.* The way Amor's head fell back in surrender beneath Stryph's onslaught punched Stryph in the chest. Amor tasted like sherbet. Stryph couldn't stop tasting him.

"Whoa."

Stryph bit back a growl over the interruption. He leaned away. His dick leaked at the vision Amor presented. He'd never seen anyone so ready to get fucked, and not only had he lived a long damn time, he'd also brutally edged for hours with willing bodies. Stryph hated turning away to acknowledge the new arrival.

Tam looked ready to bolt as Stryph focused on him. It was rare for guilt to penetrate his hard shell, but he didn't like himself when Tam looked scared.

"Sorry," Tam said like he'd been zapped with a cattle prod.

Risk appeared behind him. "Why are you apologizing?" He sounded pissed.

Tam showed a sudden strength, surprising Stryph as he stood taller. "I accidentally interrupted them," Tam explained, motioning their way. He flashed them a sweet smile. "Sorry, again. We're just passing through. Please ignore us and go back to what you were doing." He looked away and took Risk's hand, leading him toward a willow tree as if nothing happened.

Stryph shook his head.

Amor chuckled, bringing Stryph's gaze back his way. The laughter in his expression fascinated Stryph.

Stryph cleared his throat. "Well." He sucked in a breath as Amor brushed his fingers down Stryph's stomach, heading for a much harder place.

"You'd better tell me how to get to your place before we give anyone a real show."

For a moment, Stryph didn't move. He stared at Amor with all the hunger in his heart before nodding. "Agreed." He still didn't move away. Not yet. Stryph brushed his lips across Amor's once more before walking away and circling the car without a backward glance. He was afraid if he kept staring at Amor, he would snap. It wasn't as if he cared if anyone watched.

It wasn't until Amor started the car and his headlights swept across the tree Risk and Tam had disappeared beneath that Stryph decided he needed a distraction. "Every time I've been here, Tam has stayed in that same spot. He seems to have an odd fixation with the outdoors."

Amor nodded as he steered down the drive. "Tam is part mage. His magic will lure him to connect with the earth. Plus, he spent many years in captivity."

Stryph stared at Amor's profile. "How do you know all this?"

Amor shot him a quick wink. "I read his heart. Which way am I going?"

Not his mind. He'd read Tam's heart. That was an interesting gift. "Left." He waited until they were three miles from Jonathan's before snapping his fingers and changing the scenery. Streetlights appeared on either side of the road, lighting the path. Everything had a different hue here. The buildings were old but had a high-class charm.

A hum came from the back of Amor's throat. "Interesting. It makes sense you wouldn't live in the human realm."

Stryph shrugged even though Amor wasn't looking his way. "It's one thing for me to visit Jonathan's or my best friend, Shepherd. Otherwise, like Jonathan, I don't much pass for human." His eyes gave him away. They were more iridescent than not. While his form might be human most of the time and he could change his appearance, he couldn't always hide his eyes. Nor did he want to pretend to be anything other than himself. While Stryph no longer set his wings free, since there was no need for them here, he didn't wish to be human either.

"Is Shepherd human?" Amor's question distracted Stryph from his musings.

"He's an alpha mate, and a vampire mate, but yes."

"Interesting." Amor didn't say more. Stryph would be damned if he dug.

"It's the next right turn."

Amor followed Stryph's directions until he steered his way down Stryph's cobblestone driveway. He parked behind the five-story stone townhome next to Stryph's car. He chuckled. "I see you sent your car home."

"Of course," Stryph said, slipping from the car. "I trusted you would be true to your word and spend the night."

"This is a nice place," Amor said, ignoring Stryph's claim. "Even though light is suppressed here, you've kept the old world feel."

Stryph flashed Amor a smile as he led him to the door. "The old world was a better world. Everything was built by hand when humans took pride in their work. Of course, the place has some modern touches too."

"Naturally." Amor was so sure of every word

Stryph spoke. It was... nice. Shepherd was the only person who'd shown any trust in him before now. It seemed showing faith in him was what did it for Stryph. Possessiveness grew inside him, mixing with his hunger. Amor was dangerous. A fact that became more apparent by the moment as Amor shoved his way beneath Stryph's black t-shirt while Stryph opened the back door. His arms encircled Stryph from behind. He stroked Stryph's stomach before unbuttoning his jeans without preamble. Stryph wasn't sure they'd make it upstairs to the bedroom. Then, Amor tore open Stryph's zipper and shoved his hand down Stryph's underwear and Stryph knew they would not.

With a twist and a pull, Stryph had Amor inside with his back against the closed door. He tore at Amor's clothes, listening to them rip. They could go slow later. He had a madness scratching at his brain only being inside Amor could assuage. Amor tugged at Stryph's clothes with every bit as much enthusiasm. Stryph let Amor have his shirt before he dropped to his knees and swallowed Amor's cock. His scalp stung as Amor tugged at his hair, pulling him closer, and fucking his mouth. There wasn't a single part of Amor that didn't taste sweet—like he'd been sculpted from sugar. Stryph couldn't get enough. He used his spit to easily pump his fingers inside Amor's ass. Only when Stryph was certain his mind would snap from need did he fly to his feet. He gripped Amor's ass and easily lifted him from his feet. Amor held on to his shoulders with his back against the door. His head fell back as Stryph impaled him. Moans filled the air.

Stryph didn't go slow. This wasn't making love. He fucked Amor with all the desperation that lived inside him. He kissed and bit every place he could reach as he slammed inside Amor. The sound of skin slapping skin mixed with whimpers, making Stryph hotter by the second. Amor felt perfect on his dick. Tight and hot. Amor scratched at Stryph's skin and pulled at his hair, driving Stryph mad.

A loud cry tore from Amor. He painted their chests and stomachs with cum. Stryph saw stars at the first spasm around his cock. The pressure that had been threatening his crown burst from him in an explosion that nearly took out his knees. An inhuman sound ripped from his throat as he pumped Amor full of cum.

His strength never wavered as he rode the last waves. He kept Amor pinned to the door, kissing his throat, and hiding his face. Stryph knew he couldn't let Amor see his expression. Sometimes, he was too dark, even for himself. Amor had blown Stryph away. His passion matched Stryph's perfectly.

A sweet smell seemed to linger around them. Stryph's lungs felt heavy. Each breath he took labored, even though he didn't need to breathe. Then, Amor gently stroked his hair. Something happened to Stryph's chest. There was an odd flutter —like butterflies. His eyes stung. He held Amor closer, needing more of something unnamed.

Amor chuckled, sounding like a sexy angel. "I believe we've established you don't suffer from little dick disease, but I think we should run more tests."

A laugh burst from Stryph. Happiness exploded through him, taking him by surprise. He couldn't recall anything like the emotions pouring through him. Stryph couldn't let Amor escape. With a final kiss, Stryph scooped Amor into his arms and headed for the stairs. He had a week. Stryph would make it count.

———

STRYPH'S HOME SMELLED GOOD—LIKE WOOD AND polish. Just like the town, his furniture was indeed from an older time. Antique. Sturdy. Built to last. Stryph's bedroom was one entire floor of the gray stone townhouse. It was open and the huge bed in the center of the room was definitely the focal point with its four posts and maroon coverings. One wall was solid wood shelves and rods—like an open closet. The only door in the room led to the bathroom. That wasn't an amenity people like them needed, but Amor had always loved baths and showers. With all the house had to offer, Amor was only interested in one thing beneath its roof—Stryph.

Nude, Stryph looked exactly like the weapon he was built to be. Tall, sleek, and well-defined. Amor hadn't expected to fall upon the man the moment they crossed the threshold. He regretted nothing. Their bodies weren't like humans. They didn't need air, food, water, or gentle care. Amor didn't need to be stroked and lubed. He couldn't be harmed. Amor only needed exactly what Stryph had given him —release.

Stryph was an enigma. He'd taken Amor hard and fast against the barely closed door while tearing at Amor's skin with his teeth. Yet, now, he sat in a jetted tub filled with hot water and bubbles while feeding Amor strawberries dipped in dark chocolate. Stryph had facets. Amor had grown tired of food so long ago he couldn't recall when he'd last tasted anything. From Stryph's fingers, Amor hadn't tasted anything better in his life than the fruit Stryph offered. Especially since Stryph kept stealing kisses between each bite, as if he only fed Amor so he could taste the strawberries on Amor's tongue. Amor hadn't decided if the move was loving or greedy. Either way, his dick hadn't gone soft since that kiss by the car.

Stryph's sexy gaze held Amor's stare. "Have I earned your trust enough for at least one confession from you?"

"Ominous," Amor said on a chuckle. "Ask your question, and then I'll decide."

Water splashed over the edge of the tub as Stryph managed to shift even closer. He adjusted Amor's weight straddling his lap. "Those flowers you gave Jonathan, we both know they would survive this world's version of a nuclear blast. Why did you lead them to believe they must spend the week reveling in one another to ensure the plant's survival?"

"That was Celeste. The Hellish clan never rests. While that's a necessary evil, they're burning out. She wants them down for a week."

Stryph looked truly interested in knowing everything Amor could tell him. "Is that why you're staying too? To ensure they stay down for a full week?"

"That's two questions. You've only earned one."

"I also helped you find Jonathan," Stryph reminded him.

Amor released an exasperated huff he didn't really feel. "You owed me that much for breaking my car."

"You flattened my tire. That made us even," Stryph shot back.

"It was the intent behind your breaking my car that decidedly does not make us even."

Stryph didn't look the least bit repentant. "It was desperation."

A snort escaped Amor. "You've never been desperate a day in your life."

Stryph's expression shifted—like a mask fell. Amor was left staring at the deepest sadness he'd ever seen. His throat tightened at the sight. "That's not true in the least, sexy."

Amor found himself leaning in—like an invisible force pulled him closer. He held Stryph's gaze until the final moment. His eyes fell closed as their lips met. Emotion filled his chest as their tongues brushed. It was a sweet tasting. Amor held Stryph's face between his hands and savored every shared moment. Stryph's fingertips slowly traced the line of Amor's spine with the lightest of touches. He didn't try to take control. Stryph let Amor lead. Almost as if he luxuriated in the sweetness of the moment.

Amor wanted more of the sweetness. After kissing a path from Stryph's lips to his ear, Amor buried his face in the crook of Stryph's neck, scooted as close as he could get, and rocked. The friction between their bodies was nowhere near enough, yet it was perfect. A stuttered gasp came from Stryph's throat, driving Amor. He moved slow, holding Stryph while rotating his hips, riding him. Their cocks moved against each other while trapped between their bodies. They were making love. Amor felt that to his core. He'd gone into this night expecting to taste Stryph's darkness. Amor imagined he would before it was over. For now, he wanted this —a connection in the making.

Stryph didn't take control. He relaxed and let Amor have his way. It was nice. Amor liked the slow build. He lightly sucked and nibbled on Stryph's neck as he let the pressure build. The way their erections barely brushed forced Amor to focus on that and nothing else. He lost himself in the moment. Nothing mattered except the man beneath him. Stryph made a noise somewhere between longing and begging. Amor worked harder at pleasing him. He rode Stryph a little faster, sloshing water over the tub's edge. His balls drew up tight. Amor turned wild, openly using Stryph's body to get off. He ground against Stryph, reaching for the explosion that beat against his crown, and begged for release. In a blinding flash of light, an orgasm struck. Cries ripped from Amor. The room spun, and the scenery changed. Amor found himself beneath Stryph on Stryph's massive bed. Their mouths clashed and their tongues battled, stroking each other. Stryph's huge body moved against him, seeking release. Amor clawed at Stryph's skin, demanding his cum. He wanted to drown in it.

Stryph tore his mouth away. With teeth bared, he openly strained against Amor. Amor never blinked. He seared the memory into his brain, determined to remember this moment forever. There was so much beauty in the erotic. Everyone was at their purest and truest form in these moments. Amor had never seen anyone as blindingly gorgeous as Stryph was as he covered Amor's chest in cum. Amor feared for his heart in that moment as he recognized the truth. Stryph had the power to break it. Amor wasn't sure he didn't want him to try.

FOUR

ONE THING HAD GONE EXACTLY as Amor suspected after a night with Stryph. He could still feel where Stryph had been. Amor was a god, and he was sore. He caught himself smiling over the idea for the hundredth time. The scent of coffee wafted through the air, dragging Amor from the bed. He was feeling lazy, but he also hadn't tasted coffee in ages. Plus, Stryph was waiting for him. Amor could feel him. A shimmer from the corner of his eye snagged Amor's attention. The huge mirror covering half a wall, swirled—like a pebble had been tossed into a pond. That was all the warning Amor got before a massive blond man stepped through. He was tall, wide, and solid, but his blue eyes were kind. His soul was soft and fluffy—like he was the softest place in the world to land.

His gaze locked on to Amor. Shock crossed his features before a blush exploded across his face. He spun, turning his back on Amor's nudity. "I'm so sorry. Usually, I let Stryph know I'm coming. I didn't expect... We were supposed to meet last night, but this explains a lot. Stryph never stands me up. Not that it matters. We're only friends."

Amor shook his head and waved his hand. Jeans and a t-shirt appeared, covering his body. "You must be Shepherd. I'm sufficiently covered now."

Shepherd peeked over his shoulder, as if Amor would lie. He turned once he confirmed Amor's claim. "You're right. I'm Shepherd. Again, I'm so sorry. This has never happened before. Stryph doesn't usually bring people here. I'll shut up now."

No matter how hard he bit his bottom lip, Amor couldn't fight his smile. Shepherd was obviously very nice. "I'm Amor," Amor said, hoping if he met Shepherd halfway then Shepherd would feel a bit more at ease. "There's no need to apologize. You say Stryph was supposed to meet you last night?"

Shepherd nodded. "At Raff's."

Amor turned up the power on his charm,

blatantly using it to set Shepherd at ease. "I'm afraid that's my fault. He came to my rescue."

"As long as he's okay, he doesn't owe me any explanations. I just worry over him a lot, because... well, it's complicated. But I'm glad to meet you. More than you know, maybe."

It was as Stryph said. This was his best friend. It was obvious he'd seen the darkness inside Stryph as well. The loneliness. "Stryph has told me a little about you. I haven't run across many humans who are strong enough to be mated to an alpha wolf and a vampire. Celeste has blessed you. I would love to know more. Why don't we have dinner tonight? Bring your mates. What are their names again? Stryph and I will buy."

An instant smile snapped to Shepherd's lips, making him breathtaking. He had such a happiness inside that Amor fought the urge to touch him to see if he could feel it too. "Raff and Dante. And Stryph doesn't believe in paying for things."

"Meh," Amor said, waving the statement away. "I will pay. Human money is nothing." He snapped his fingers and a stack of bills appeared in his hand. He tossed them away, and they disappeared before raining down on them.

Shepherd's smile never abated. He shook his head. "Is it considered rude if I ask what you are?"

Against his will, Amor smirked. He gave a short bow while holding Shepherd's stare. He let his abilities show in his expression, becoming temptation incarnate. "I am Amor, son of Venus."

"Whoa." Shepherd cleared his throat. "Um. Wow. Well, I guess I should get back to my mates. We'll come back in a bit, after the sun sets, and take you up on that dinner offer." He glanced behind him at the mirror, as if already picturing his mates nude. "It was nice meeting you."

A soft chuckle rumbled from Amor as Shepherd practically leapt through the mirror in his race back to his mates. He knew he should feel a little guilty, but he didn't. Amor was riding the high of a night with Stryph. He couldn't help but feel like everyone should be getting just as lucky. Damn, he'd forgotten what it was like to be here, unmuted. He needed to find Stryph, now that he thought about it. He was kind of hungry again.

FROM HIS SPOT LEANED AGAINST THE KITCHEN counter, Stryph watched Amor descend the stairs and move around the room. He was sexy. Stryph couldn't tear his eyes away. Unfortunately, Amor seemed to be gathering his things to leave and Stryph couldn't have that. Especially since the sexy god had barely looked his way today.

"What are you doing?"

Amor's emerald gaze swung his way. "Getting ready."

A wave of panic rose inside Stryph. He carefully kept his features blank. Stryph wasn't ready to be dismissed. Left alone. "Tired of me already, huh?"

Amor's musical laughter floated through the air. "You're coming too."

Stryph's eyebrows rose without his permission. "I am?"

Abandoning the chore of finding the strips of last night's clothing, Amor crossed the room. He plucked Stryph's cup from his hand and set it aside before stepping into Stryph's hold. "Don't you want to have dinner with Shepherd?"

"Really?" Even Stryph heard the hope and happiness in his voice. "We're having dinner with Shepherd?"

"Yep." Amor punctuated his answer with a kiss to Stryph's chin. With a happy sounding hum, Amor came back for more, nibbling on Stryph's chin. His lips moved to Stryph's throat. "Mhmm, I like this spot too," he mumbled as he gnawed on Stryph's neck. He finally leaned away. "While I was getting dressed, Shepherd stepped through the mirror. That's a lot of trust on your part, by the way, giving someone unlimited access to you like that. I couldn't pass up the chance to know someone better who's earned that level of trust. So, I asked him to dinner. He seemed a little surprised, to be honest."

Stryph imagined Shepherd was downright floored and would have tons of questions. "To be fair, we usually warn each other before crossing the mirrors, but I forgot I was supposed to meet him last night. He was probably worried... or enraged."

"Worried," Amor said with a shrug, clearing up any misgivings on the topic. "He said you'd never stood him up before."

"Damn." He hated disappointing Shepherd. "I was a little distracted." Even Stryph heard the lust in his voice. "I ran into this sexy god who stole my breath before kidnapping and molesting me."

With an outraged sounding huff, Amor pushed away from Stryph. "Maybe I should just go then, since I had to kidnap you to get your attention."

Stryph plucked Amor from his feet before he made it two steps. "Okay. You win." He placed a loud and wet kiss on Amor's nape. "I did the chasing and the kidnapping. The only thirsty one in this scenario was me. Let me know when I say what it takes to keep you here."

Amor disappeared from his hold. There was no warning. One second Stryph held the world. The next, he was gone. Before Stryph had time to absorb the fact that Amor was gone, he reappeared in Stryph's arms, except they were now eye to eye. "You only need to say one word and I'd give you anything." The claim sounded soft and from the heart. Stryph couldn't look away.

"Tell me, and it's yours."

Amor slowly lured Stryph closer. His gaze never wavered from Stryph's "Please," he whispered.

"If you insist," Stryph said, claiming Amor's mouth.

The outraged growl Amor released against Stryph's lips only made Stryph hotter. Amor had already proven he could disappear in an instant if he liked. The fact that he didn't said more than any disgruntled sounds.

Amor tore his mouth away. He panted as Stryph continued kissing his jaw. "How long do we have until sunset?"

"Maybe half an hour," Stryph answered against

Amor's skin.

"That's when Shepherd will be here."

Stryph froze with his lips still pressed against Amor's neck. He calculated time against his wants. Fuck it. "I can do it," Stryph swore, going for the button on Amor's jeans.

"Agreed," Amor said, snapping his fingers and making their clothes disappear.

Stryph nodded. "Good thinking." He swept Amor from the floor. Amor wrapped his legs around Stryph's waist. Their lips met with the same fire that raced through Stryph's veins. The more he had of Amor, the more he wanted. It was like a sickness had taken hold of him. He wasn't sure if a week of this would be enough. Hell, Stryph wasn't sure eternity would be long enough.

THEY CHOSE A RESTAURANT ON STRYPH'S SIDE OF the realm which did nothing to lessen the awkwardness of the meal. Shepherd and his alpha, Raff, were the only two who still ate. Everyone else only ordered to make the pair feel less on display. A fact evident by the way everyone else moved the food around on their plates without actually eating a bite.

Amor got down to the business of getting to know Shepherd. After all, that was why he was there. "So, Shepherd, are you happy?"

Shepherd froze with his fork halfway to his mouth, as if he'd expected a million different questions than the one he'd been handed. "Yes." He sounded questioning, but not because he wasn't sure if he was happy. Instead, it was as if Amor's question confused him.

Amor nodded. "Good. That's all that really matters in life. People worry too much about work and hundreds of other day-to-day things but being happy is the only real concern anyone should have."

Shepherd set his fork aside. "Oh. That's really nice. I never thought of it that way, but you're right."

Stryph stroked his knee beneath the table, capturing Amor's attention. When he glanced over, the heat in Stryph's stare blasted him. Amor pressed his hand to his stomach. He'd never had such a strong connection with anyone. Stryph felt the same. Amor could feel it. They exchanged a knowing smile before he focused on the throuple once more. Amor caught them obviously holding a mental conversation. Even though he couldn't hear a word, they still used their hands. Amor chuckled at the sight. Three sets of eyes turned his way. Each filled with guilt.

Shepherd was the one to apologize. "Sorry. We get lost in ourselves sometimes."

"I like that description." It warmed Amor's insides. "It always seemed to me that shared thoughts would get annoying."

Dante cocked his head to one side, as if he found Amor's words curious. "But you're a god. Can't you read all minds?"

"Most likely."

"Most likely," Raff repeated. "Don't you know?"

"Well," Amor said, lifting his hands for a moment before dropping them back to his lap as he searched for the right words. "I mean, that's rude, reading other people's thoughts."

Three sets of eyes blinked at him as if he was some strange breed of dragon they'd never seen. Shepherd was the first to break. "What about if you meet your fated mate? Won't you want to share thoughts and have that mind connection?"

He was sweet. So innocent. "Gods don't have mates, but—even if we did—it would still be rude."

All three heads turned Stryph's way, as if the move had been choreographed. "A penny for your thoughts," Raff said, joining the conversation.

"Yes, I can read minds. No, I don't do it often. It's rude."

Amor bit back a smile and reached for Stryph's hand beneath the table. Their fingers linked.

Shepherd leaned closer. "Aren't you worried about other gods reading your mind, if everyone can do it?"

"No. I'm too strong." Shepherd looked more confused than before Amor answered. Amor decided to expound. "I keep my thoughts blocked from others."

"Doesn't that get exhausting?"

Amor lifted one shoulder in a half shrug. "It becomes such a habit that I don't even think about it unless I want someone to hear my thoughts."

Once again, all the heads turned Stryph's way.

Stryph chuckled. It was sexy. "Same," he said before they could ask.

"This is fascinating," Shepherd said, sounding genuinely interested.

Amor found himself shaking his head. "I'm surprised you don't know everything about our world. Celeste found you strong enough for an alpha and vampire mate. Plus, you're besties with this guy." He stroked his hand down Stryph's arm.

Stryph's laughing gaze turned his way. "Did you

really just use the word bestie in reference to me?"

"Do you deny it?"

"No."

Damn. He was gorgeous and Amor couldn't get enough of touching and teasing him. "Well, then. If the shoe fits, gorgeous. Lace it up and wear it with pride."

Stryph's laughter made every ridiculous thing Amor said worthwhile. After another exchanged humorous glance, they rejoined the rest of the table. Three sets of eyes looked at them with matching surprised stares.

They think I've been abducted by aliens.

Stryph's thoughts brushed across Amor's mind with the most loving of touches. Amor was swept away by the sensation. He'd never met anyone who could break through his wall and fuck... Amor was a little frightened by how strongly he felt already, and how badly he wanted more.

Maybe you have been.

A low chuckle rumbled through Amor's mind. It wasn't his. Stryph had heard him. He pressed his hand to his stomach again. This feeling of being more to Stryph than anyone else had ever been, it filled Amor with such greed. This was the one who would break Amor. He already felt the growing heartache, and they still had a few days left together. In that moment, he wished he'd never let Stryph into his car. Stryph's touch and laughter, they would haunt Amor forever.

⸺

THE SENSATION OF AMOR STROKING HIS stomach had Stryph floating on cloud nine. The moment they'd gotten home from dinner, they'd stripped, and climbed into bed. They hadn't done anything except hold each other. It was odd. It was sweet. Stryph didn't do sweet. Yet, he couldn't recall ever feeling so much at peace, or happier. He prayed this moment never ended. Stryph didn't believe in wishes, but Amor was his first. He prayed he could keep this one good thing for himself.

"I'm super curious. You can look like anything or anyone at any time. What made you choose this exact form?"

Stryph was pretty certain there was nothing Amor could ask that he'd refuse to answer. Every question meant Amor wanted to know him. That's the only reason Stryph chose to be honest about this particular question. "I guess it was around twelve hundred years ago, I was floating through a battlefield at Edington as a heavy fog, spreading unrest and stirring the blood for oncoming war. This Viking warrior was sharpening his battle axe. Mid stroke, he froze. His head lifted and his eyes locked on to me—like he saw me. Not like he saw drifting fog—he saw me. It was the first time I'd ever been stricken dumb by anyone's beauty. I was... moved. So, I took his form. I've kept it since then, and I'd never come across another who matched his impact on me... until I met you."

A soft chuckle caressed Stryph's throat. "Why did you have to go and ruin such a great story by ending it on a lie?"

Stryph sprang, rolling Amor beneath him. Amor was still smiling despite Stryph's irritation. "Are you trying to spark my fury?" Even Stryph heard the accusation in his tone.

Amor's wicked grin grew. One sexy shoulder lifted in a half shrug. "Maybe."

A wave of dark hunger rose inside Stryph. It died a swift death as Amor lightly stroked Stryph's bare hip. Stryph lowered his head and brushed his lips across Amor's. "I think I'll keep my temper to myself," Stryph whispered as he stole another kiss. "You're a little too used to having your way."

An outraged huff blew across Stryph's skin. "Are

you saying I'm spoiled?"

It was Stryph's turn to shrug. "If the shoe fits."

Amor's hands ran down Stryph's back before cupping his ass and squeezing. "I do love shoes, so..."

"So..."

"What's a guy got to do to get ruined for all others around here?"

Stryph's thoughts skipped a beat. He knew Amor had meant the words to be playful, but the question still punched Stryph in the throat as realization hit. Stryph wasn't sure about the exact combo of actions to ruin someone for all others, but he very much feared that Amor had already done it. One thing Stryph never did was share his bed with anyone for more than one night. Not only had he already done as much with Amor, Stryph didn't want to stop. He wanted Amor to stay.

THE WAY STRYPH STARED AT HIM ALMOST MADE Amor regret his question. He thought he'd like the darkness Stryph offered, but he'd never expected the way Stryph looked at him now. Amor felt a real spurt of fear. Like he was in danger, but maybe not in the way he expected. The thing was, it wasn't really sex

Amor was after. Not that he'd complain if things went there. Amor wanted to push and see Stryph's every facet.

"What if I decide to torture you?"

Amor already felt a bit tortured. He licked his lips before realizing how the move gave away his nervousness. "Maybe I'm into that."

"We'll see," Stryph said, lowering his head. At the last second, he changed angles and buried his face in the crook of Amor's neck. The lightest kiss, one Amor had to strain to decide if it was real, brushed across his neck. It was followed by another and another until Amor was so hard, he was in pain. He wasn't one to lie there and take it. Then again, he didn't want the moment to end.

Stryph shifted. He draped Amor's leg over his forearm and held it higher, making room for himself between Amor's thighs. Stryph's lips continued skimming Amor's skin. He rocked. His cock skimmed Amor's asshole, just teasing him with the slightest friction against his most sensitive skin. Pre-cum leaked onto Amor's stomach as he fought not to blow right then. He'd never had anyone tease him into an orgasm like this. All Amor could do was take it. Pleasure held his body hostage. Stryph kept up the gentle rocking, doing nothing more than using

Amor's crack for his own pleasure. Yet, Amor's cock acted like Stryph was focused completely on it.

Amor gripped two handfuls of the sheet and held on, trying not to fly apart. "Stryph." The whisper fell without Amor's input. It was his heart crying out.

"Beg me."

Coming from anyone else, Amor might have left at the demand. He didn't need anyone else to find pleasure. This was different. This was more than wanting an orgasm. He needed Stryph and the connection he'd never felt with anyone else. "Please?"

The word barely died on his lips before Stryph shifted positions again. His cock, slick with pre-cum slid up Amor's length. A gasp caught in Amor's throat as an orgasm shook him. Stryph's mouth covered his, smothering the sound. Amor's entire body glitched out of his control as Stryph kissed him. Amor poured his heart into their kiss, trying to make Stryph feel what he felt, even though Amor couldn't give his emotions a name. Amor already knew, one day, he'd be on the edge of sleep and the ghost of Stryph's lips on his skin would strike, leaving him wrecked. He didn't know how he was supposed to walk away from something this powerful. He wasn't sure he was that strong.

FIVE

THE TREE LINE grew thicker the closer Stryph got to Jonathan's. He lost himself in the drive. Stryph could've zapped there and been there in an instant. That's probably how he'd go home. For now, he needed the time to think. Amor had ordered Stryph away, sending him to take Jonathan to get some real clothes. If anyone had ever given him an order he'd followed in his entire life, Stryph didn't recall it happening. This one he'd jumped to fulfill. It was Amor. Stryph wanted to make him smile.

His chest hurt. Stryph couldn't explain the phantom pains or find a cause. In truth, he was afraid to look too closely. He was scared he'd find exactly what he suspected—he'd be heartbroken when Amor was gone. For a moment, his thoughts turned so black, Stryph almost regretted driving after all. Maybe he shouldn't spend time alone with himself. The iron Hellish gate came into view, saving Stryph from himself. He forced his mind blank as he turned down the drive.

Halfway to the house, Jonathan appeared in the passenger seat. "Oh, my gawd. I'm so excited." He somehow managed to be on his knees, twisting in every direction like a little kid and almost putting out Stryph's eyes with his wings. "How fast does this car go? Wait. Can we get to magic stores in a car?"

Stryph fought the see the driveway around Jonathan's wings. Giving up, he stopped. He managed to shove Jonathan's wing aside in time to see a very pissed off looking Niall storming outside. He was obviously trapped by the daylight and unable to dissipate. Niall stopped beside Stryph's door. "You cannot go without a guard, Jonathan. I never agreed to that."

A loud sigh rose in Stryph's throat. He rolled down the window. "Don't worry. We're not driving."

Jonathan's wings fell. "Oh."

He looked so crestfallen that an unexpected wave of sadness washed over Stryph. "I thought we'd take the mirrors," he explained. "That way you can find your way back, in case you'd like to go again."

Jonathan tried for a smile. It was fleeting. "Okay. I don't get to go anywhere anymore, since I don't look human." His gaze moved toward the house. It was obvious he didn't want Stryph looking at him. He fingered one of his feathers as his wings engulfed him, as if he was protecting himself. "Before this, I used to travel all over the world. I haven't left this house in over a year."

A round of cursing so intense it raised Stryph's eyebrows ranted outside Stryph's window. Stryph stared at Niall's open fury in horrified fascination. He'd never seen anything quite like it. Finally, Niall stopped and focused on Stryph. He set his fists on his hips and his nostrils flared. Niall looked like a man on the edge of murder. "I expect you to bring him back in the same condition he left in. Give me your word that you'll protect him with your life."

"Of course." Because the world needed Jonathan, and Stryph couldn't survive without this world.

Niall gave him a sharp nod. "Have fun." He turned and headed for the house without a backward glance.

Stryph put the car in reverse. It seemed they were driving after all. "I'll explain how to get there by using the mirrors later. It's not like I'm going anywhere."

Jonathan's smile made the concession worthwhile. "Okay."

As Stryph backed up and turned around, he wondered if he was going soft. He couldn't imagine ever caring about anyone's feelings in the past. Then, he'd met Shepherd. That's who he chose to blame as he drove. Shepherd was the soft choice. Otherwise, he'd have to blame himself... or Amor. Fuck. He was in real trouble. Thankfully, Jonathan's excitement was distracting. He looked ready to jump from the car. It was cruel to keep someone like him trapped inside the Hellish property. No doubt, Cin and Niall did everything in their power to keep him happy, but still. A gilded cage was still a cage.

Stryph snapped his fingers. The scenery transformed. Jonathan twisted, looking in every direction. Stryph counted himself lucky that he didn't lose an eye this time. Jonathan wasn't very self-aware of his size.

"The buildings are so pretty here. It reminds me of a picturesque town I once visited in Northern France."

Stryph thought the description fitting. The place did look closer to European than American. "You said you used to travel all the time. What had you on the move?"

Jonathan settled down. "Work. I used to be an investigative journalist for a worldwide magazine in New York."

A spurt of curiosity ran through Stryph. He realized how little he knew of the human version of Jonathan. "Seriously? How did you go from that to this?"

"Fate," Jonathan answered, as if that was always the answer. Stryph supposed it was. He sometimes forgot how trapped everyone else was to fate's whims. Stryph was free, and yet, he wasn't. "I'm not unhappy." Jonathan's claim brought Stryph back from an edge inside his mind. It was never a good thing to look too closely at himself. "At least, I don't think I am." Jonathan laughed. "Honestly, I'm usually too busy to think about it. What about you? Are you happy?"

Stryph blinked. Until Amor had made a point of asking about Shepherd's happiness, he'd never considered that people didn't ask that unless they had a beautiful heart. Unfortunately, he wasn't the type of creature who should be looking too closely at his cheer meter. "I am today, yes."

"Ten bucks says that's Amor's doing." The

playfulness in Jonathan's voice might've bothered him if he wasn't so enamored, but there it was.

Stryph cleared his throat. "We're here," he said, pulling up in front of his usual clothing shop. He had to stop this conversation before it went any deeper. Jonathan seemed like he was the happy type. Stryph was not. Sometimes, he had to recognize his danger to others and leave them alone.

Without Stryph around, Amor found himself wandering from room to room, feeling lost. He'd thought he would be fine while Stryph took Jonathan shopping. In fact, he'd been the one to insist Stryph go today. He hated that Jonathan had spent so much time stuck in a kilt for lack of normal clothing for their kind. Seriously, he loved Celeste, but she was wrong for leaving Jonathan to muddle through alone the way she had.

An hour into pacing, Amor knew he wouldn't make it. Closing his eyes, he focused on the Hellish property, or rather, the hole in the map where it should be. The air changed. The warm sun caressed his skin. When he opened his eyes, he was standing outside the iron gate. Amor headed down the driveway on foot. Since he wasn't met by wolves, Amor assumed he was a little more welcome this time. Before he made it to the house, he spotted Tam along the with the wolves and discovered why he'd been left alone. Amor covered his mouth with both hands to hold in the laughter. Around a black cauldron, stood Tam, Evan, and Bleidd—all of whom looked to be glued together.

"For the tenth time, I don't know how it happened," Tam cried, sounding distressed. "I followed every step Baptiste gave me."

"By all the powers of Odin, if we ever get out of this..."

Amor jumped to intervene before Bleidd finished that thought and ruined his relationship. "May I be of some assistance?"

Three heads swiveled his way.

Tam smiled like he wasn't glued hip to hip to Evan. "Hi, Amor."

"Fucking hell," Bleidd growled, sounding deadly. "We're fucking trapped like this and any damn body could be attacking the property."

"To be fair, I'm not here to attack anyone." Amor couldn't keep the bright note from his voice.

Evan was the only one who looked truly distressed. In his defense, he was the one trapped in the middle. "I'm supposed to be protecting Baptiste. Why would he give us a spell to practice that locks us together? Everyone already thinks I'm too young to be the guardian of a god's mate."

Bleidd visibly tried to keep his temper in check to spare his mate's feelings. "Everyone knows you're the best guardian wolf ever. This was probably just Baptiste messing with you."

Amor shook his head. He wondered how long they'd been stuck like this. Amor snapped his fingers and set them free. "There. No harm done."

With his head down, Evan walked away without looking back. Tam looked crestfallen as he watched him go. Bleidd turned his face up to the sky, visibly praying for strength before going after his mate. They disappeared into the woods. Amor wasn't sure what to do.

"Should I come back another time?"

Tam looked devastated as he turned inward. His expression immediately brightened. "Oh. No. You're good. Evan is okay. He just shut me out because Bleidd tracked him down and attacked." He blushed. "Risk is sleeping, and it seems I'm done practicing magic for the day. What do you want to do?"

Amor closed the distance between them and peered inside the cauldron. It was empty. "Let's practice your magic," Amor suggested. After all, he wouldn't always be there to unlock people's legs.

———

THE MORE TIME STRYPH SPENT WITH JONATHAN, the more he liked him. He was upbeat, smart, and funny. Stryph understood why so many beings felt free to bring him any problem. Watching Jonathan flit from store to store had been an adventure in itself. Shop owners, while accustomed to serving powerful beings, hadn't met anyone as affluent as Jonathan. They bowed and scraped to make him happy. Not that it was hard to please Jonathan. He was overjoyed just to be out of the house. Trying on a shirt that accommodated his wings was like watching a kid get ten Christmas mornings. Everyone stared at Jonathan everywhere they went. Even this side of the realm, most people had never seen a Nephilim. Jonathan being king was just icing.

By the time they were—once again—traversing Jonathan's driveway, Stryph had learned more than his fair share about the Hellish clan. But the most important tidbit Stryph had gleaned was, Jonathan loved his clan and this world. Celeste had done well.

Stryph spotted Amor, taking turns dancing

around a cauldron in the yard with each member of the clan. A chuckle escaped Stryph with no input from his brain.

"You love him."

Stryph's head whipped around at Jonathan's claim. "That's taking things a bit far."

Jonathan waved dismissively at himself as he gathered his bags. "All-knowing. No sense in lying." Jonathan met his stare. "You're not weak. He is literally love in its purest form. I'm not sure it's possible to touch him and then expect not to feel him. Demons curse. Gods bless. Either way, touching one or the other will get in your head. What did you expect would happen?"

What had he expected? It was a legitimate question.

Jonathan grabbed the door handle and paused. He looked Stryph's way and flashed him a wicked smile. "Just so you know, he loves you too. He just hasn't accepted it as real yet." Jonathan threw open the door and dropped a final bomb as he leapt from the car. "He also expects you'll break his heart."

Stryph's throat swelled. If touching Amor was love, touching Stryph was hell. No doubt he'd tainted something good. His gaze moved back toward the party raging around some magic spell. The tightness in his chest eased. Amor looked happy here. He could keep Amor smiling. All he had to do was convince Amor to stay. He could do it, right? Stryph had to. He wasn't sure he had another choice.

As Stryph climbed from the car, Amor's laughing smile turned his way. Somehow, Amor managed to brighten even more. He waved at Stryph. "Hi. I got bored without you and decided to come for a visit." He met Stryph halfway. As he went up on his toes for a kiss, Stryph automatically bent to meet him. Their lips brushed like it was the most natural thing —as if they belonged together.

"What did I miss?" Stryph asked, motioning toward the crowd of dancers.

Amor linked arms with him and steered him toward the cauldron, but he lowered his voice like he was keeping the conversation between them. "Well, it seems Evan has been having trouble with his magic lessons for a while now. I believe he burned down part of a voodoo shop a while back, and today he delivered a message wrong. Tam ended up cursing them with some crazy form of leg lock when he tried deciphering the spell inside the message. So, I decided to help. We've been working on brewing a frivolity potion. It, of course, takes a party to make a party, so the guys agreed to help."

Stryph looked around, taking in all the smiles. "You make happiness everywhere you go, don't you?"

Amor hummed. "Mhmm. That's a nice thing to say. Will you dance with me?"

"There's no music."

"Do you need a beat to move your feet?"

A laugh escaped him at Amor's ridiculousness. He swept Amor off his feet, held him to his chest, and walked him toward the rest of the dancers. "For you? I'll see if I can get these ancient hips moving." Stryph couldn't look away or stop smiling as Amor tossed his head back and roared with laughter. He knew Jonathan was right. There'd never been a chance he would touch Amor and not feel him. Even as jaded as he was, Stryph recognized the beauty of what he held. He would do everything within his power to protect it.

SIX

AMOR COULDN'T BELIEVE it was his last day. They'd spent it together in New Orleans, walking along the river and checking out the shops. Stryph had kept his sunglasses in place so Amor could sightsee among the humans. They'd held hands while talking about everything and nothing. Amor swung between abject happiness and debilitating sadness. He'd never felt closer to anyone. No one had ever felt so out of reach. He was paralyzed by his emotions. Things felt so much stronger here. The intensity of everything was terrifying. He could barely think about leaving without a hole opening in his gut. The closer the time came, the more he felt.

"You look like you've enjoyed this trip," Stryph

said over his shoulder as he opened the door for Amor.

Amor waited until Stryph closed the door behind them to respond. "This has been a great week."

Stryph tossed his keys on the kitchen table and turned Amor's way. He closed the distance between them, towing Amor against him. Stryph held Amor's hips between his hands, massaging. He looked more intense than Amor had ever seen him. "What if you stayed?"

Amor swallowed past the lump of fear that immediately formed in his throat. He never expected this from Stryph. "What do you mean?"

Stryph didn't look away or back down. "What would happen if you just stayed... with me?"

"Are you asking?"

It was Stryph's turn to look nervous. "Maybe."

Amor couldn't upend his life over a maybe. Stryph was amazing. Amor would miss him and think about him for the rest of eternity. He also imagined his heart would break without Stryph, but Stryph didn't want him for good. Not really. Amor was safe in Heaven. He had his home and garden. Here, he had nothing but Stryph and Stryph would eventually get bored.

A sad smile tugged at the corners of Amor's mouth. He touched Stryph's cheek while letting his feelings show in his eyes. "My place is in Heaven, and yours is here. Can we just enjoy this? I don't know about you, but I don't connect with people often. Nor do I get a ton of joy from life. This has been a unique week for me. I don't want my last night to end on a sad note."

Stryph kissed the tip of Amor's nose. "Okay. I get it."

Amor held Stryph's face between his hands, refusing to let him get away. It hurt even more than expected, losing Stryph. Words he couldn't express choked Amor. He hadn't expected Stryph to ask him to stay. Amor hadn't anticipated having to refuse such a temptation. The realization he would never see Stryph again after tonight crashed down on Amor's head, suffocating him.

"It's okay," Stryph repeated. He shuffled closer and brushed his lips across Amor's. "I'm not good. You're better off in Heaven." He hugged Amor, holding him tight against his massive chest. Amor couldn't function. He let everything happen to him. The shattering was real. It paralyzed him. There were millions of things he wanted to say—things he would regret not saying. His lips wouldn't work.

Music, soft and sweet, filled the air. Stryph kissed the shell of Amor's ear. "This is the dance I want," Stryph whispered, pulling Amor closer and leading him into a slow dance. He didn't give Amor a chance to pull away and fall apart. Amor followed Stryph's lead. The mood changed a little more by the second. Stryph kept stealing light kisses every place he could reach while Amor soaked in every touch. He needed Stryph to take away the pain.

Stryph's hands slipped beneath Amor's shirt. He stroked Amor's sides, moving higher. Amor lifted his arms, letting Stryph have the shirt. Stryph tossed it aside and went back to moving to the music. Amor found himself fingering the buttons on Stryph's shirt. He slipped the top one free before moving to the next. Amor didn't hurry. This would be the last time he was allowed to do this. Amor swallowed hard at the thought. After tonight, undressing Stryph would be someone else's job. In a month or two, maybe Stryph wouldn't ever think of him again. It would be like he didn't exist.

The two halves of Stryph's shirt fell open, exposing his flawless torso. Amor let everything fall away as he pushed the material down Stryph's arms. Stryph watched his every move. His intense focus was like a physical touch. With Stryph's shirt gone,

Amor stroked the hard lines of his stomach before moving to the button of his pants.

"Will you think of me sometimes?" Amor didn't mean to ask. The question slipped out through the cracks in his heart.

"I'll think of you always." The honesty in Stryph's voice had Amor going for a kiss. He needed to taste the promise on his tongue. Without thought, he bit Stryph's bottom lip. Stryph exploded. Amor's back hit the wall hard enough his head bounced off the wood even as Stryph collided with his chest. It was only right things should end where they started —in this kitchen. He didn't want Stryph to make love to him again. His heart wouldn't survive it. Amor needed Stryph to leave his mark—scorch Amor's nonexistent soul.

With a single thought, Amor had them nude. He needed Stryph's firm ass filling his hands. His nails scored Stryph's skin as Amor hauled him even closer. Stryph dipped his head but didn't go for Amor's mouth. Instead, he sank his teeth into Amor's shoulder. A loud moan vibrated from Amor as Stryph broke the skin. He wanted to hurt on the outside like he ached on the inside. Amor yanked Stryph's hair, forcing the man's mouth to his.

Stryph's kiss was violent. It was exactly what Amor needed.

"Take it away," Amor begged, needing Stryph to make the pains in his chest stop.

In a flash, Amor found his cheek pressed against the kitchen table. A cry tore from his throat as Stryph's cock filled his ass. His fingers encircled Amor's throat. He squeezed as he tugged Amor back against his chest as he fucked him deep. Amor lost himself in the brutal sex he craved. His body was on fire. The pressure built and pulsed. Even as he came harder than he had in his life, Stryph didn't stop. He simply changed positions and kept going, dragging more and more pleasure from Amor.

Stryph's storm went suddenly silent. His lips lightly brushed the shell of Amor's ear, sending chills down Amor's body. "I don't want you to take the pain away from me. You're the closest to alive I've ever been."

The final piece of Amor shattered in his chest. He would love Stryph until the end of time. Coming here was the cruelest thing Amor had ever done to himself. He would feel Stryph even once the memory of them no longer existed for Stryph. As Amor turned in Stryph's arms, determined to make love to him, Amor fully understood for the first time that love didn't always make things better. Sometimes, it killed everything good.

SEVEN

JONATHAN PACED THE FLOOR, feeling restless and irritated for no reason at all. Out of pure boredom, he grabbed the remote. He couldn't even remember the last time he'd watched TV. It didn't feel relative to his life any longer. Today, though, Jonathan felt driven. There was something ugly in the air. A cloud of despair.

He flipped through the channels, finding news program after news program. They were all more of the same—one horrible headline after another. Twenty people missing after a group hiking trip. Wars breaking out in other countries. Several hate-based laws being passed or voted upon. Lost children. Blah, blah, blah. It all left Jonathan feeling heavier by the moment. Nothing was right. The world was so out of balance that Jonathan could practically sense the dissention in the air like a physical thing which it was, really. The realization had Jonathan shifting through the world in his mind, connecting with the earth, and understanding the recent poison. Stryph's pain washed over him, knocking the air from his lungs. He fought to breathe.

Bring everyone. Shepherd too.

Aye, my king.

Jonathan wished Dougal's quick response made him feel better. He wasn't sure they weren't all completely fucked. Amor's presence in their plane had taken Jonathan's guard down. He hadn't been paying attention like he should. Now Amor was gone. The imbalance of things was beyond a level he could control. There was no controlling Stryph. Jonathan only had one plan, and it was beyond bold. It was suicide.

The room filled with body after body. His mates came first, looking worried. "Are you okay?" Cin asked, rushing to join him on the couch.

Jonathan found himself trying to smooth out the frown line between Cin's eyebrows. "I love you."

Jonathan nearly choked on the words. His chest hurt. Stryph's pain clouded everything.

Before Cin could respond, Baptiste, Eirik, Kallus, Evan, and Bleidd filled the room. Risk and Tam followed on their heels. Shepherd and Raff appeared in a flash of light with Dante carrying them. Lire, Dougal, and Faolan brought up the rear, having gathered everyone. All eyes were on Jonathan. He could feel their worry. He knew they could feel the black clouds rolling in too.

He didn't waste time getting to the point. There was no time to waste. Stryph's pain could take out a small government in the blink of an eye. "No doubt everyone has felt the unrest. It's stirring everywhere. It's only a matter of time before the world explodes into an all-out war, or the demons sense their time to strike while dissatisfaction is at its highest. We have to act."

Baptiste shook his head. "What can we do about a general discord? We can't control the overall ugliness of life."

"This is more than the usual unrest. It's Stryph."

Baptiste shook his head. "I thought he'd somewhat friended your clan. Evan talks about him as if he is the decent sort. Why would he suddenly shift his favor away from humans?"

"We don't believe it's purposeful," Cin answered for Jonathan, reading his thoughts.

Shepherd nodded along. "He's heartbroken. I was worried this would happen. The way he looked at Amor at dinner the night we went out." He shook his head. "I knew Amor didn't intend to stay, but damn, they looked at each other like it was real."

"Damn," Eirik cursed, summing up all Jonathan's feelings. "A heartbroken weapon of the Gods. No good comes of that."

Jonathan sensed his time to strike. "It's time to do something extreme. I have us hidden. No one, not even Celeste can see or hear this meeting. If anyone wants to leave, do so now, so you can still claim ignorance of this conversation." No one budged. Jonathan gave them a sharp nod. "Good. Stryph is one of our own, and he needs us to go completely off the map to help him—literally." He met Eirik's stare. "We need to get into Heaven and kidnap Amor." Even Jonathan recognized he asked too much. He sounded crazy. Jonathan didn't care. If Amor wanted to deny his love, Jonathan couldn't make him acknowledge his feelings, but he could try.

Eirik's face didn't as much as twitch. If he thought Jonathan was insane, his expression didn't show it. "Let me get this straight. You want me to get you into Heaven so you can kidnap a god?"

Jonathan didn't sugarcoat things. "Well, not me, personally. I'm not going. Stryph is—if he agrees, but yes."

"All right." Jonathan blinked at Eirik's immediate agreement. Eirik didn't stop there. "Best we move quickly then. We don't want to give any of the gods time to see us coming."

Jonathan shook his head. Shock owned him. "I have to be honest. I didn't expect you to be onboard with this, but I love you for it."

A huge grin spread across Eirik's face. "Better a stout heart than a sharp sword. It's been a long time since we've seen battle."

Jonathan cast a look around the room. Everyone wore a smile similar to Eirik's. It was a room filled with warriors. Still, Jonathan needed everyone to agree. "There's still time if anyone wants out." When no one spoke up, Jonathan motioned Shepherd's way. "We'll take the mirrors. You'll have to lead the way."

Shepherd did hesitate. He moved to the large antique mirror that hung in the living room. He took a keychain from his pocket, touched it to the glass, and turned it into a shimmering pool.

Jonathan brought up the rear as his clan stepped through the mirror. He hoped he wasn't signing their death warrants. If the worst came, he would take Celeste's wrath to the extent he could, and hope it was a fair trade. Jonathan kept telling himself the sacrifice was for the entire world, but he knew the truth. He risked everything for a man who'd not only almost killed him once, he might not even like them that much. But Jonathan believed in love. He felt in his gut that one emotion would save them all. He had to believe, or all else was lost.

From his spot on the bed, Stryph stared at the opposite wall, seeing nothing except the visions in his head. Over a week ago, he'd climbed into an empty bed. He hadn't moved since. It wasn't necessary for him to do anything. He wasn't human. There were no trips to the bathroom. Food and water were unnecessary to him. He didn't require showers or brushed teeth. Stryph was only a solid form when he chose to be. Everything worldly was for the living. He was nothing to everyone. Yet he was everything to everyone. It was a life he wouldn't wish on anyone.

He'd been insane to offer to share this existence with Amor. Amor was too good for Stryph.

Stryph stared so long in the direction of the mirror it took him a second to realize it shimmered like a pool. He wanted to feel something. Anything. Not a hint of emotion penetrated his mood. He was done. It was time to hibernate and let the world do what it did. His presence would still linger. Stryph just wouldn't be conscious to make the judgement calls. People would survive. Humans always found a way to endure. He was the one left to suffer alone with nothing but the dark cloud of himself. It was time to choose sleep. He had thousands of years of naps to catch up on.

Shepherd stepped through the mirror, closely followed by his mates. Before he could work up any feelings over Shepherd bringing guests without his input, more people followed. Tam, Risk, Evan, and Bleidd poured in. Three people he didn't know followed shortly by Dougal, Faolan and Lire. A hint of exasperation rose inside Stryph but didn't take root. His limbs felt too heavy. Finally, Jonathan, Niall, and Cin brought up the rear before the mirror returned to its solid state.

Stryph eyed the crowd inside his bedroom. "Is this an intervention?"

"Nay," Cin said, speaking up for the group as they nodded along.

One of the strangers with jet black hair and shimmering blue eyes stepped toward. "This is a coup d'état."

A derisive snort escaped Stryph. "No need to overthrow me. I'll gladly pass you my powers. You'll beg to give them back."

Tam crawled onto the foot of Stryph's bed and bounced. "No, silly. We're about to break in to Heaven and steal Amor. He belongs here with us."

Stryph's eyebrows tried hitting his hairline. "That's a bold plan for a room full of creatures no more capable of getting to Heaven than I am." Stryph looked away. He couldn't stand their stares. "Not that it matters. Amor doesn't want to be here. I've lived long enough to know that you can't kidnap someone and force them to love you."

An evil sounding chuckle fell from the demon, Lire's lips. "Well, now. That's not true at all. How do you think I won Dougal?"

Jonathan made an impatient gesture. "We don't have time for this. I can't keep us hidden from Celeste forever without drawing suspicion. Amor loves you. I can see it. That's what's important here.

Fate favors the bold. Time to be the badass you are. Let's go, Stryph."

Despite not wanting to get sucked into this obvious non-plan, Stryph sat up. "Even if Amor chose me, which he won't, since he's already told me no, this insane plan is pointless. We can't take the stairway to get to heaven, no matter how many songs humans write about it."

Another of the strangers stepped in. He was Evan's twin in almost every way, except it was only in looks. Stryph saw his shell for the mask it was. "I am Eirik, son of Heimdall. Keeper of the door to the Heavens." Hope rose in Stryph's chest as Eirik spoke the words Stryph needed above all others right now. "I can get you in to see Amor."

"Don't you want to try?" Shepherd asked, making Stryph's eyes burn. "Don't you need to know that you've done everything to win him? Can you live with knowing you didn't fight for him?"

"Please?" Tam said, bringing Stryph's gaze his way. "He loves us. I know he does. Don't let him leave us."

A loud sigh escaped Stryph. He looked closer at the clan surrounding his bed. They were all warriors from different times ready to go to war with Heaven for him. He shook his head. "You're all completely insane." Tam's face fell and Stryph couldn't take it. He tossed his legs over the side of the bed. "I guess it's as good of day as any to die. What's the plan?" As Stryph said the words, a fire lit inside him. If this worked, he was moments away from seeing Amor again. If it didn't, maybe someone up there would finally put him out of his misery. Either way, fuck it.

Eirik's smile was wickedness come to life. "I thought to take you straight to Amor—snatch and grab before any lightning bolts fry our asses."

"In," Stryph said with a sharp nod. Asking Amor nicely hadn't won him anything. Maybe leaving him no choice would do the trick. After all, Stryph liked chains. Stryph's smile grew. Even to him it felt evil.

Eirik moved closer. "Get in and get out. Take my hand."

Stryph accepted. With Stryph's palm in his, Eirik closed his eyes. Stryph swore he could feel the man's focus. His skin warmed. In a flash, everything changed. Eirik was gone and Stryph stood alone in the dark. The silence was deafening. Amor stood only feet away in the sunlight, staring at the most beautiful garden Stryph had ever seen. He looked sad. Stryph needed him. It was like he was in a cage. A shimmering wall of water separated Amor's sunlight and Stryph's darkness. It was like a line had been drawn in the sand. Dread rose in Stryph's chest. Eirik was gone. Something wasn't right. Things were too easy. Yet, they weren't. All he had to do was step through the water and Amor would be his. Stryph didn't hesitate. He leapt with nothing more than faith and love in his corner.

His garden didn't need him. Everything planted here thrived in Heaven. Before now, he hadn't realized how useless he was here. There was no one to teach magic, take to dinner, or make him burn. No one looked at him like they'd starve without his kiss. Amor stared at his flowers and felt nothing, except empty. He was broken without Stryph. It was no one's fault but his own. He didn't know how to fix it. Stryph was probably past any infatuation he'd felt. It didn't matter that Amor could still feel Stryph's final kiss lingering on his lips. His fingers moved to his lips without thought. He ached.

"Amor."

Amor spun at the strangled sound of his name in a voice he'd never expected to hear again. For a moment, he thought his loneliness had snapped his brain. Stryph stood in his garden, looking as sexy as

Amor remembered. There'd been a small part of him that wondered if he'd only built Stryph up in his mind. No. He was beautiful. Amor's spurt of overwhelming happiness died as swiftly as it hit. Stryph was in true distress. He looked like he was drowning on dry land. No sooner than Amor had the thought than water poured from Stryph's mouth and he crumpled to the ground.

Amor raced across the garden and dropped to his knees. Stryph didn't need oxygen to survive, but—for whatever mysterious reason—Stryph was openly drowning. Water poured from his body, pooling around him. Amor tried lifting his head, unsure of what to do. "Stryph. Holy crap. I don't know what to do. Why are you here? How are you here?"

Stryph stared at Amor with his heart in his eyes, even as he fought death. "Came for you," he choked out around the water.

Celeste appeared at his side in an instant. "Take him, Amor. You have to get him out of here. The heavens are safeguarded against the fallen. He'll die if he stays."

Amor didn't hesitate at those words. Fuck what would happen to the world without Stryph. Amor wouldn't survive without knowing Stryph existed. He scooped Stryph from the ground. His wings grew, lifting them into the air. In an instant, they were bursting through the cosmos before crashing through the human realm and appearing inside Stryph's bedroom.

As his feet hit the floor, Amor glanced down, expecting Stryph to be back to normal. He was unconscious. Amor glanced around in a panic. Jonathan's clan stood waiting, as if they'd been there all along. Maybe they had been. Amor was too scared to think.

"Begone from me," Amor screamed, sending them away with only the power of his voice. He couldn't handle their worry on top of his fear. Amor dumped Stryph on the bed before straddling his hips and lightly smacking at his cheeks. "Stryph. Breathe or whatever it is that keeps you here. Don't do this to me."

Nothing. He wasn't dead, but neither was Stryph there. It was as if his essence had retreated to some place safe. Somewhere Amor couldn't hurt him anymore. That one thought had Amor's throat swelling. Stryph had come for him. In heaven. He'd risked everything to chase after Amor. Fight for him. Was being safe really the better choice? Was it so important to him to be surrounded by the familiar?

With no other choice left to him, Amor settled

onto Stryph's chest. He didn't know how to help, so he held Stryph with his wings draped over them for warmth. Amor would stay as long as it took to reach him. A hot tear slipped from Amor's eye before falling onto Stryph's chest. Amor loved Stryph. He didn't want to lose him.

THE SUN BEAT ON STRYPH'S FACE, MAKING HIS cheeks sting. Still, he couldn't turn his face away from the heat. His eyes opened. Green leaves swayed with the wind above him while bright beams of sunlight cut through the branches. Peace filled him.

"I used to come here a lot."

Stryph turned his head. Tam sat beside him. "It's quiet."

Tam nodded. "It's never quiet in Hell. You'd think—eventually—you'd learn to tune out the constant noise, but no. That's part of the torture."

"How long were you there?" Stryph felt like he should know, but something was missing. His thoughts were scattered. He felt barely there. Like something really important was missing.

"Years." Tam looked different—harder. The childlike qualities that made him irresistible were missing. He had a frightening edge to him today. "It felt like a century. Every day was something new and horrible until I lost every ounce of humanity."

"I couldn't look at you and tell it now."

Tam's mouth lifted in one corner in a sardonic smile. "That's all Risk's doing. It's terrifying to me to think of him falling in love with me when I look closely at things. Maybe I could've killed him instead of loving him back. He's a lot surer of me than I am."

Despite his scattered thoughts and confusion, Stryph liked talking to Tam. He didn't feel so alone. "Do you still fear you could harm him?"

"Yes." Tam's honesty blew Stryph away. But Tam didn't stop there. "Maybe one day I'll stop being able to live with the internal screams and I'll finally find a way to make it stop for good. That would destroy Risk. I already don't sleep anymore for thinking about it." Tam hugged his knees to his chest. "I'm not good."

I'm not good. Those words niggled at the back of Stryph's mind. Hadn't he said them recently? "You're good. If you weren't, you wouldn't worry about anything. I would know."

Tam nodded while staring off in the distance. "Maybe. How long do you plan to stay here?"

Stryph looked around. There was nothing but

empty fields of grass around him. "I don't know." He didn't know where here was.

Tam touched Stryph's forearm, bringing Stryph's gaze back his way. Things were getting darker. Not like the sun was setting, but like everything was fading away. Tam held his stare. "If someone can love the soulless animal that crawled out of hell, Amor can love you." At the sound of Amor's name, pain exploded through Stryph's chest. Tam faded a little more. "You're breaking his heart. He's waiting for you."

He thinks you'll break his heart. The faintest memory of Jonathan speaking those words floated through Stryph's mind. The world plunged into darkness and fear swept through Stryph. He was missing a huge piece of himself. It had been ripped away. Before a full-blown panic attack set in, warmth settled over him. The phantom sensation of a kiss brushing his ear had Stryph reaching to hold on to it.

"You can't leave me alone here."

The words sounded like they came from a distance to cut through Stryph's heart. A sweet scent tickled his nose—like sherbet. Stryph worked to get closer to the source. His mouth watered. He'd tasted that. It tasted like the one true love of his life—like Amor.

"I love you. I'm so sorry I was too scared to stay."

Stryph fought a spurt of irritation. Amor shouldn't be apologizing to anyone. "Shhh. I love you, baby."

"That's it. Come back to me, angel. I'm right here."

The warm weight covering his body had Stryph's attention. His eyelids felt like they weighed a ton. He fought to get out from underneath them. When a sliver of light hit his eyeballs, he hissed against the sight. Warm lips brushed his jaw, making him try harder. Fluffy gray feathers surrounded him. They looked so soft. Stryph couldn't stop himself from stroking them. A moan against his neck had Stryph's head turning. Emerald green eyes waited for him. Love stared at him. Memories slammed into him. He'd broken into Heaven. He'd found Amor in his garden. That was the last thing he remembered. He glanced around. They were in his bed. Amor's wings kept them warm.

"How did we get here?" His voice sounded rough—like tires through gravel.

Amor stroked his cheek—like he couldn't stop touching Stryph. "The safeguards put in place to keep out the fallen almost killed you. I brought you home."

Stryph looked away. He wished Amor hadn't. "You should've left me. I don't want to keep doing this alone."

Amor sniffed, bringing Stryph's gaze back his way. His gorgeous green eyes were full of tears. "You're not alone. You have me."

"I don't. You left me." Stryph still wasn't sure he wasn't imagining Amor being there. Maybe his mind had snapped.

"I shouldn't have. It was stupid. I've been suffocating without you, but I was scared to come back."

Each second that ticked by, Stryph's strength returned a little more. "Why?"

A tear finally lost its battle and spilled over Amor's lashes before rolling down his cheek. "I was afraid you wouldn't want me anymore since I left."

Stryph's throat swelled. His voice showed it when he spoke. "I'll always want you. By whatever miracle, I think you're meant to be mine."

Amor nodded. "I know."

Those two words lit a fire inside Stryph. Hope flared for the first in ages. He licked his lips, scared to ask. Stryph had to know. "Does that mean you'll stay?"

Amor nodded.

A burst of energy fueled by happiness had Stryph rolling Amor beneath him. Amor's laughter bounced from the walls, making Stryph's heart smile. "Don't fuck with me here. Are you really staying?"

Amor's smile slipped away but the happiness in his eyes didn't dim. "As long as you'll have me, I'll stay."

Happiness turned to need. Stryph couldn't survive another second without Amor's kiss. He lowered his head. Amor's head shot up, meeting him halfway. In that moment, Stryph understood. Amor felt every bit as strongly for him as Stryph felt for Amor. This wasn't a case of a fluke meeting at a backwoods pool hall. They were exactly where they should be. Cool air brushed his suddenly bare skin, making him realize Amor had stolen his clothes. A chuckle rose in Stryph's throat and vibrated through their kiss.

We have zero boundaries.

Amor's sexy laughter rang through Stryph's mind. *We should probably talk about that.*

Later, Stryph agreed. Right now, he was overjoyed to have nothing standing in the way of making love to his sexy god. As much as he loved pain, he didn't want that right now. He needed an act of promise, solidifying them. With a single thought, lube coated Stryph's fingers. He toyed with Amor's ass, easing the way for his cock.

"Nifty trick," Amor whispered against his lips.

"I'm full of them." The words died on as gasp as Stryph pushed his way inside. No one moved him like Amor. He knew Amor didn't recognize his power. Amor didn't know, Stryph wasn't like this with anyone else. Sex for him was blood and flesh. This wasn't sex. It was touching something beautiful. A connection to a missing piece of himself. A piece he desperately needed.

"Stryph." The desperation in that single word was like a punch in the gut. Stryph wanted to hear it over and over until the end of time. Amor's short nails scored Stryph's back as he strained against him. "I love you," Amor cried as his hot cum filled the space between them.

Stryph realized, he hadn't imagined things earlier. Amor truly had admitted to loving him. He could barely contain the power of that knowledge.

"I'm not done with you yet, my sexy angel. You should buckle up."

A huff of laughter brushed his shoulder as Amor kissed Stryph's skin. "I can take it."

Stryph thrust deep. "Good. I'm about to test that." He kissed Amor's ear. "I promise, you'll feel how much I love you too by the end." He felt Amor's happiness and relief wash over him, as if they were his emotions. They were more connected in mind than Stryph had ever realized before. That was a sign from the gods. This was a blessed union. They weren't imagining things. This was real. He would do everything in his power to deserve them. Until there was no life left in him to share.

EIGHT

HEAVEN WAS QUIETER each time Amor returned. He recognized that it was him. Amor could no longer swallow the silence. Even he wasn't sure when he'd stopped finding peace here. Amor had been around long enough to know; peace came from within. His tranquility rested with Stryph now, but he needed to do this too.

Celeste appeared in Amor's garden shortly behind Amor, as Amor knew she would. "Yes, I promise I will keep a close watch on your lovely flowers and won't let them die. And no, I'm not upset with you for choosing to leave. You've always been free to live in whichever realm you like."

A smile tugged at Amor's lips. "Is this really how you plan to play this one, Celeste? As if, I chose?"

Celeste's brow furrowed. "I don't know what you mean."

Amor sighed. "Okay," he said dragging the word out. "I guess I won't bother thanking you then, since you are completely innocent in all of this."

A musical laugh filled the air. "Way to stoke my pride, Amor. Sometimes I forget how good you are at twisting people's arms. Fine. Did I think you might meet Stryph during your trip? Yes. Did I set you in his path? Possibly. Am I the least bit ashamed over my interference? Not at all. Matchmaking is my thing. I set them up, you sweep them off their feet. That's always been the way of things." She curled her nose. "Be honest, you're not really surprised, right? You know I can't stay out of things, and you were discontent here. You have been for a while."

Amor tore his gaze away from the explosion of color in his garden and stared at the dark haired and emerald eyed goddess who ran everything with grace and ease. "I didn't know I was unhappy until I was happy."

A sad smile touched Celeste's lips. "I know, but Stryph knew. Each and every day, he was aware of the misery of his life. It grew and grew." Amor's throat swelled a little more with each word. He couldn't tolerate knowing unhappiness had ever touched Stryph. "He couldn't keep waiting for you forever."

Amor blinked at the words. "Waiting for me?"

Celeste nodded. "Everyone is meant for someone, even the gods. Love and strife go hand in hand, keeping the balance. He was created for you. But you've been here, oblivious to his pain and longing. All you knew was something was missing from you, but you didn't know what. Stryph has been painfully aware of what was missing from him, but not who. I couldn't let him choose sleep. If Stryph turns his back on the world, the imbalance might mean its destruction. Stryph, Jonathan, Tamil, Eirik... the list goes on and on of those who act as checks and balances. Survival depends on everyone playing their role, each and every day. It's time for you to play yours." She winked and leaned closer. Her eyes flashed with mischief. "That doesn't mean you can't enjoy your place, right?"

Heat flooded Amor's cheeks. Blushing was completely out of character for him. There were many perks to Stryph. He cleared his throat. "I hope I'll still be allowed to visit."

"Of course," Celeste said without hesitation. "Your heavenly membership card hasn't been revoked. You've merely had a change in address." She shook her head. "Unfortunately, discord has no place here, so Stryph will not be permitted to come along. I'll come to him soon though. It's been too long since I visited. By the way," Celeste said, waving her hand dismissively and looking away. "Make sure my grandson understands he hid nothing from me. I can't let him have all the credit for such a perfect coup."

She truly had a streak of the devil in her. Sometimes it amazed Amor.

Celeste glanced over and smiled, obviously hearing his thoughts. "Well, the devil is my brother after all. You can't fight your genes. I only hope he has a streak of me left in him too."

The hint of sadness in her voice tugged at Amor's heartstrings. They were friends, after all. "Give me one last hug, then," Amor said, waving her forward. "I'd hate for Stryph to start thinking I abandoned him again."

Celeste rushed forward and squeezed him hard. Amor overflowed inside. She'd done something amazing for him. Amor would never forget it.

Stryph solidified outside the Hellish gate and headed up the drive. He found Tam exactly where he expected, sitting by the cauldron. He smiled as Stryph plopped down beside him.

"You showed up just for me. I don't think that's ever happened."

"Apologies. You deserve a better friend."

Tam's smile brightened. "We are friends, aren't we?"

Stryph had a true soft spot for Tam. "Of course, we are. Is it okay if I ask you something?"

"Yes." Tam looked a little nervous—like he worried what Stryph would ask.

"Does Risk know why you stopped sleeping?"

Tam immediately reached for his doll. The move almost had guilt sneaking in, but sometimes friends had to speak up. "No. He thinks I'm working on my magic while he sleeps."

Stryph cast a quick glance toward the cauldron. It was cold and Tam didn't have any supplies with him. He took a breath. "I know there's nothing anyone can say that'll take away ingrained fear, but you're so damn strong. Seriously. You're easily one of the strongest beings I've ever met. Risk is so lucky to have you."

"I'm the lucky one," Tam cut in. He looked away,

blushing. "He doesn't see me the way other people do." Tam twisted his doll. "I'm not good at explaining things... He thinks I'm pretty." He blushed again. "To look at," Tam added, unnecessarily.

Stryph was having a hard time not laughing. Tam was adorable. "Risk is not the only one who thinks that. He's just the only one who matters to you."

Tam met his stare, and Stryph realized something. No one ever looked at him as dead on as Tam. Tam wasn't scared of other people at all. He was frightened as hell of himself. "He thinks I'm pretty on the inside too."

"He's right. You're beautiful and you won't ever choose to leave him. Would you do something for me? A favor?"

Tam nodded. So serious. "Of course."

"Go to bed with your mate. If you get there, and you get scared again, I'll be here waiting. We can hang out all day, if you'd like. But if you get in there, and you fall asleep, or realize you're much happier just being with Risk, stay. Just go in there and give him your faith. Believe in his belief in you. I know that you know you can trust him above anyone else. Would Risk love a weak man?"

Tam didn't answer right away. After a minute, he

finally shook his head. "Risk is too strong to be attracted to someone weak."

"There you go," Stryph said, straightening his spine. "He's definitely extremely attracted to you." Stryph bit back a chuckle when Tam blushed again. "Go to your mate." Stryph settled onto his back in the grass. "I'll be right here if you need me."

Tam didn't move right away. He stared at the house while biting his lip. After a minute, he sprang forward and kissed Stryph's cheek. He didn't say a word as he gathered his doll and headed for the house. Stryph stared at the sky and smiled. He would stay, because he'd said he would, but Tam wouldn't be back. Tam loved his mate. He would work hard to keep Risk happy, even if that meant rearranging his dark thoughts to match Risk's brighter image of him. That wasn't the only thing that had him smiling at the sky.

"That's a neat trick there. How did you manage to zap straight into this lovely compound?" Even Stryph heard the laughter in his voice as he stared up at his unlikely mate, hovering in the sky above him.

"That little peck on the cheek was adorable. You truly love these people, don't you?"

Stryph rubbed his chest. "Are we not answering each other's questions today? I didn't know."

With a sexy sounding chuckle, Amor nimbly dropped to the ground. Stryph opened his arms for Amor to settle against his chest. "As it happens,"—Amor scooted close and settled his head on Stryph's chest—"there's a list you must be on to zap into the property. It seems a while back, the Hellish clan had a bit of a problem with people appearing unannounced directly inside the house. So, Jonathan put a bubble around the property. If you're on his list, you can still pop in. I imagine it won't be long before you're added."

Stryph released a fake huff of exasperation. "I took the man shopping and returned him to his mates in the same condition I found him in."

He felt Amor nod against his chest. "I'm aware, but I heard a tale that you almost killed him once."

"For fuck's sake. It was an accident. He tried pushing into my mind. I pushed back a little harder than intended. Everyone lived."

"I know, sweetie," Amor said, stroking his stomach and obviously humoring him. "His mates haven't quite forgiven it yet."

Stryph brushed his knuckles up and down Amor's arm as he stared at the sky. He got it. If anyone hurt Amor, they wouldn't be easily forgiven... if they lived. "I do love these people," Stryph admitted, answering Amor's earlier question. "They are quite unique. Did you enjoy your visit with Celeste?" Stryph said, changing the subject.

A sexy hum vibrated from Amor, brushing Stryph's chest. "Mhmm. It was informative. Did you check on Eirik?"

"I popped by his mate's voodoo shop before coming here. According to Evan, who I didn't know worked there, he's perfectly fine. It seems, when Eirik tried escorting me to Heaven, I was catapulted to you while he never moved. So, there's that."

Amor's touch moved a little lower, distracting Stryph. "Well, he has no reason to fear Celeste's wrath. The whole thing was entirely her plan."

A smile tugged at Stryph's lips. He wasn't the least bit surprised. Stryph had felt her hand in things. "She did good," Stryph praised, knowing she would hear, as well. Amor kept stroking him. Stryph's eyes fell closed. Peace settled over him. He couldn't recall the last time he'd been this content doing nothing at all. Amor's lips brushed his throat and his fingers dipped beneath Stryph's waistband. Well, maybe he could be a little more content. He was willing to let Amor try to please him more, from now until the end of time.

Please consider leaving a review at the retailer where this book was purchased. Reviews really help with a book's visibility, which ensures I can continue writing. Thank you, Charity.

ABOUT THE AUTHOR

Charity Parkerson is an award winning and multi-published author with several companies. Born with no filter from her brain to her mouth, she decided to take this odd quirk and insert it in her characters.

*Eight-time Readers' Favorite Award Winner
  *2015 Passionate Plume Award Finalist
  *2013 Reviewers' Choice Award Winner
  *2012 ARRA Finalist for Favorite Paranormal Romance
  *Five-time winner of The Mistress of the Darkpath

Connect with her online:

--Join my street team:
facebook.com/TeamCharityParkerson
--Sign up for my newsletter: http://
bit.ly/CharityNews
--Website: charityparkerson.com

--Facebook: facebook.com/authorCharityParkerson
facebook.com/TheMenofSin
--Twitter: twitter.com/CharityParkerso